SILVER LINING

THE SILVER COVE SERIES

JILL SANDERS

GRAYTON

One of the hardest I've ever had to write…

To Zach…
Your spark burned too quickly.
May your soul travel the universe spreading
stardust and sunshine everywhere you go.

Missing you

CONTENTS

SUMMARY

Sarah has always been torn between two worlds—the carefree, easygoing world of her hippie mom, where life is all about helping others and building good karma, and the real world, with real responsibilities, like paying bills, and getting to work on time, values obviously gleaned from dad's side of the family.

She has nothing but fond memories of her father. He was always there for her and clearly loved her mother more than she thought possible, despite mom's overtly eccentric behavior. Losing dad was tough, and Sarah's been reduced to being the girl with the crazy mom, a reputation that's not likely to increase her chances of landing her dream promotion at the resort across the bay. Especially with the new competition. Ben is an attractive, sophisticated, and savvy businessman, clearly there to destroy her chances of getting the job. Her luck couldn't be worse.

With an obvious attraction and closeness forming between the two, Sarah discovers that Ben's motives may not be as clear as she first thought. What's he really doing there? Is she being played?

Benjamin Rothschild has come to the popular upscale resort strictly for business. There to evaluate Sarah for a new position, he can't help being drawn in by her sensual charm and free-spirited nature. But for some reason, this passionate beauty has it out for him. What has he ever done to her?

With so much confusion and something obviously lost in the translation, he'll have to do everything in his power to convince her that his intentions for her are true.

CHAPTER 1

There was no way he was going to have enough time to get everything done and catch the five o'clock train heading north from Boston. Ben glanced around the empty office building and felt like banging his head against a wall. Instead, he laid his forehead on the cool wood of his desk and groaned a little. For the past two days, he'd been fighting off a cold, which had caused him to fall behind on his work.

He would have had time to play catch-up that weekend if his boss hadn't called shortly before he'd left yesterday with a surprise. He'd been informed that he'd be spending the weekend and possibly longer up north evaluating an employee for a potential raise. Sure, it was something he did, but this time, he'd almost begged to have the task handed off to someone else.

His boss had been determined, though. There was no way of getting out of the trip. So Ben had worked late yesterday and had also worked through his lunch break today just to catch up.

Raising his head, he glanced at the clock and frowned. He had less than ten minutes to make it out of the building and to the train station. There was no way. Not unless he ran, and with his head already pounding, he doubted he could stomach it.

Closing down his computer, he flipped off his light and thought about what would happen if he missed the train. He'd have to sit at the station to wait for the next train, which would mean almost three hours of complete misery. Not to mention it would put him behind schedule, once more.

He shivered as he stepped outside. Wrapping his coat tight around him, he decided to chance it and started walking at a very fast pace.

How had his life come to this? He'd been on his way in school to becoming one of the finest minds in his class. He'd been valedictorian and voted by his class-mates most likely to be a billionaire by thirty. Now, here he was with less than three years to go, still working for someone else.

He stopped at the corner and wiped his nose on his sleeve. His vision was turning a little gray, so he unbut-toned his jacket to allow the cold spring air to wake him up. Shivering, he started walking again as he glanced down at his watch. Four minutes until the train.

Picking up the pace, he jogged the last two blocks. When he flashed his transit card and checked out the board, he was happily surprised to see that the train to Freeport, Maine, had been delayed by three minutes. Glancing down, he smiled. For the first time all week, something had gone his way.

Five minutes later, he settled in a seat facing forward

and sighed. He was shivering and even rubbing his hands up and down his arms did little to warm him.

He spent the next several hours on the train drinking hot tea and trying to stay awake. He desperately wished for some medication that would help combat the flu but didn't chance taking anything in fear that it would make him drowsy.

He jolted as the train stopped and noticed that he'd finally arrived at his stop. Gathering his small overnight bag, he stepped off the train to a very cold evening. He was thankful it wasn't raining or snowing, but he wished the wind would die down. It went right through him.

After renting a sedan, he prayed that he could make it through the short drive to his destination before his head exploded.

The first five minutes, as he drove, he thought back to the moment his life had been taken out of his own hands. Then he laughed when he realized that it was the day he had been born into the Rothschild clan.

"Do you know what is involved in being a Rothschild?" his father had asked him more than a hundred times in his youth. Each time he'd answered the way he'd been taught.*

"Honor, integrity, loyalty," he spouted off like some drone.*

"Exactly. And don't forget hard work. Never let it be said that a Rothschild didn't know how to get his hands dirty."

That had been one of this father's favorite lines, even though his father would never have stooped to the level of getting dirt under his well-manicured fingernails. The Rothschilds had been upper crust for more than five generations, each one getting farther and farther away from hard work as their vast money accumulated in the banks that they owned. So, how had he gone from rich boy to being a rich man's go-to guy?

Luck. As it were. One of his father's best friends had died long ago. His friend's parents were wealthier than even his father could have dreamed. So, when their only son had died, Thompson Rothschild, the second had stepped in and given up his son to be the old man's servant.

Okay, maybe servant wasn't the right word. After all, he did make almost six figures a year working for Elite Resorts International. And he was getting to use his degree, which was icing on the top.

He really enjoyed his job, and he'd thrived the first year until he settled in the position he was in today, almost directly under the old man himself.

Of course, his father was very proud of him, which only caused him more stress and pressure.

It wasn't as if he wasn't close to his parents. He wasn't their only child, but he was their only son. Maybe that's why they had pressured him so much?

Glancing down at his GPS, he frowned when he noticed he'd missed his turn. Flipping a U-turn, he slowed the car to a crawl when he saw the small road. Soon, that road dead-ended at a dock. Switching the car off, he got out and walked over to a small sign.

"The ferry to East Haven Resort at Silver Cove only runs on demand. If you have reservations or are a guest, please call Jerry to pick you up."

Pulling out his cell phone, he sneezed and then dialed

the number that was written below. He wondered just what he'd gotten himself into.

He had to wait less than fifteen minutes before a large flatboat arrived. The gentleman who jumped down the stairs looked to be around Ben's age. His blond hair was tied back and reached the middle of his back.

"Evening." The man nodded his head. "I'm Jerry. You must be B. Rothschild." Benjamin nodded his head. "We were expecting you some time ago." The man removed the chain from the end of the dock and motioned for him to drive his car across. Ben gave the dock a second look, making sure it would hold him and the car, then walked back over to get behind the wheel.

"Make sure to throw the parking brake on. You can ride with me if you want," the man said, heading back up the narrow stairs.

Ben put the car's brake on and thought about resting his head back on the seat. But then curiosity got the better of him and he followed the man upstairs.

"How often does the ferry run?" he asked, leaning against the wall as he watched Jerry steer the boat towards the dark open waters.

He glanced over at him. "It all depends on what's going on at the resort. The season hasn't quite started yet, so it's pretty slow. We've had some weddings and parties, but nothing big. Most of the guests fly in." He turned back to his task.

"Fly?" Benjamin crossed his arms over his chest and then thought better when he lunged forward and almost fell flat on his face as the boat swayed. Instantly, sickness surfaced in his stomach.

"Sure," the man said, unaware of the fact that Ben was

about to lose the small sandwich he'd had on the train. "There's a helipad on the island. Most people fly into Freeport and charter the rest of the way over." Jerry glanced over and frowned when he noticed the face Ben was making. "You're not going to be sick, are you?"

Ben shook his head lightly, but then his stomach rolled. Rushing to the railing, he lost everything in his stomach over the edge of the boat into the dark water.

"Wow haven't had anyone do that on the way to the resort. A few lose their cookies after a late night of partying." Jerry chuckled behind his back.

The gentle sway of the boat caused Ben to stay where he was for the remainder of the trip. He wasn't one to easily get sick on a boat. He was used to taking ferry trips in Manhattan and Boston.

He knew that this time the flu had gotten the best of him and wished more than anything that he could just check in to his room and bury his head under the thickest blanket possible.

"I have a cold," he said, feeling the need to explain himself to Jerry.

"I hear it's been going around. We're almost there. See?"

Ben looked up to see a floating sea of lights just ahead of them. The lights started at the dock, where he could see there were several smaller boats docked. There was a narrow lit pathway leading straight to the four-story building. Lights shined on a well-manicured yard as several people enjoyed themselves on a huge front porch. As the ferry approached the island, he could hear laughter and music from the resort.

Richness was the first word that came to mind. Here,

wealthy people came to get away and to spend their money to be in the middle of nowhere, yet still pampered like they were in heart of the city.

He knew that East Haven Resort was one of the most prestigious getaways along the northeast coast. Even some of the top names in Hollywood came to hide away on the private island, not to mention some of the wealthiest businessmen. Weddings, parties, lifestyles of the rich and famous—it all happened right here on this little slice of heaven.

Yes, most guests did arrive by helicopter. Private ones of their own, no doubt. He felt a little foolish when he remembered all the details of the resort. This cold was really slowing him down.

"Well, I hope your stay is a pleasant one. Despite the cold," Jerry said, nodding to him.

"Thanks." Ben didn't have the energy to say anything more. He popped a few mints into his mouth and walked down the stairs to his car. He slowly pulled his rental off the bed of the boat and parked it in a small parking area. He looked around and noticed that his car was the only one in the parking lot.

When he got out, he heard someone walking on the pathway and turned to see a woman moving towards him. Her long skirt flowed around her legs and hugged her narrow waist. She was wearing a loose white button-up shirt with long sleeves pushed to her elbows. Her blonde curly hair was held back in a thin black clip, just above her ears. He noticed a pair of small diamonds, which sparkled as she moved towards him.

She stopped right in front of him. "Well, we thought you'd forgotten about us." She smiled and something inside him softened. Then he did the most horrific thing he'd ever done in his life. He passed out cold.

Sarah looked down at the man at her feet and thought for a moment that it was some sort of joke. Here was her soon-to-be boss, lying in the dirt, face down. Glancing around, she frowned and thought about kicking the man. Then, putting her hands on her hips, she sighed and realized she couldn't take her anger out on the man who was here to take her dream job.

Pulling out the small radio from her skirt pocket, she called Lilith for help.

"What do you mean he's passed out?" her friend and best employee whispered back to her.

"I mean"—she turned and glanced back up at the porch, to make sure none of the guests who were currently enjoying their wine outside had seen what had happened— "he's out cold."

"Is he drunk or something?" Lilith asked.

Sarah bent down closer to the man and sniffed. "No," she replied, getting a better look at him. His dark hair was thick and shined in the moonlight. He wore it longer than most men she knew, except for Jerry. His hair had been pushed away from his face before his face had landed in the soft dirt. Now, it fell over his forehead and his eyes, which had shut too soon for her to take notice of the color. His nose was straight and narrow; all in all, a good nose. But it was his chin that had her mouth drying. The strong line told her so much about the man.

He was stubborn, determined, and would be a great

kisser. She shook her head as she realized her eyes had moved down to his lips.

"What are you doing?" This time Lilith's voice came from directly behind her. Glancing over her shoulder, she shrugged at her friend.

"Getting a better look at him," she whispered.

"Well, we'd better get him off the ground. I just talked to Jerry, who says that the man lost everything over the edge of the ferry on his trip over here. He told Jerry that he'd been fighting a cold." Lilith moved next to her and squatted down. She blinked a few times. "Good lookin', isn't he?" Her friend smiled over at her.

Lilith was very different than Sarah. Where Sarah was a measly five foot six inches and had long wild blonde hair, Lilith reached a total height of five eleven with straight, very manageable auburn hair, which Sarah had always dreamed of having.

Sarah shrugged again. "It's too dark to notice."

Lilith chuckled. "Yeah, right. Well, we'd better see if we can carry him up without anyone seeing us."

A few minutes later, Sara whispered across to Lilith. "I bet it looks like we've just murdered him."

Lilith chuckled and almost dropped the man's shoulder. "Don't make me laugh," she hissed. "I have the heavy part, remember."

"Only because you weigh ten pounds more than me and can lift more than I can at the gym."

"You should focus on strengthening your core more than flirting with all the cute guys," her friend said, glancing over her shoulder as she moved slowly around a low branch.

"I do not flirt," Sarah whispered back as she dropped

the man's left foot. It hit the pathway with a crunch and Sarah winced when she heard the man groan. "Sorry," she mumbled towards him, then held her breath in hopes that he wouldn't wake up and fire them both.

"Do you really believe he's going to be our new boss?" Lilith asked as they cleared the pathway.

"We'll find out soon enough." Sarah pushed open the back door and groaned when she saw the steep flight of stairs that they would have to haul the heavy man up.

"There's no way," Lilith whispered. "I can't carry him up those." Her friend sat on the bottom stair, letting the man drop to the ground lightly.

"Now we'll have to pick him up again," she complained. It had taken them almost two minutes to coordinate lifting his unconscious body.

"I'm going to get Rodney or Adam."

"Don't you dare." Sarah's eyes narrowed at her friend. "Rodney needs his rest and Adam is busy making dinner for the guests. Besides, what can an eighty-year-old man or a skinny French cook do that we can't." She stuck her chin out.

"Fine," Lilith growled a little as she stood back up, taking the man's full weight as she went.

It took a lot of tries but finally, they got in sync and got the man up the stairs without dropping any parts of him. "I've got the key," Sarah said, pulling the old silver chain from her pocket. "Here, turn around." They maneuvered until her back was to the door. When she opened the door to his suite, she let out a sigh of relief. "Almost done."

"Where's his stuff?" Lilith asked.

"I guess we left it by his car." She frowned as Lilith stood at the end of the bed and pushed until the man was almost standing up. "No," she said a little too loudly, causing the man's eyes to spring open just as he started falling forward.

Sarah's shoulders hit the mattress a second before his chest hit hers, knocking her breath out in a whoosh and pinning her to the soft comforter.

Sarah saw a white streak fly through the door as Lilith made her escape.

That's the last time I trust her, Sarah thought as she looked up into the darkest eyes she'd ever seen.

CHAPTER 2

*N*ot a lot shocked Ben. Maybe that's because up until now he'd led a pretty boring existence. But being flung on top of the blonde beauty had topped his chart of surprises. How he'd gotten there, in what appeared to be his room for the night, was a mystery to him.

"Would you kindly get up? You're extremely heavy," she hissed as she tried to push on his shoulders.

He blinked a few times at the richness of her voice. "Who are you?" So many other questions flooded his mind, but this one he wanted to know first.

She stopped fidgeting and looked up at him. "Sarah Holley." She smiled slightly. "Now, if you'd be so kind…" Her eyebrows shot up as she looked at him.

He propped himself up on his elbows. "Sarah?" His mind seemed to fog over. He knew that name. "I'm sick," he said, not sure why he had to tell her this.

"Yes, so Jerry tells us." She moved to cross her arms over her chest and then frowned up at him when his chest was pushed tightly against hers. "I also got a hint when you passed out cold after meeting me." She reached up with shaky hands and touched his forehead then frowned.

He felt his head spin a little. "I…" He closed his eyes.

"You're not going to be sick again, are you?" she squealed, pulling her hand away and putting it back on his shoulder to push him away once more.

His eyes met hers and he almost laughed. "No, of course not." Then his eyes moved lower to her lips. When her tongue darted out to lick her bottom lip, he watched the movement as if hypnotized. "Why did you do that?" he asked, not sure what he was saying.

"What?" she whispered.

"Touch my forehead?" he asked as she shifted under him. He felt his body react to the closeness of a beautiful woman.

"To see if you have a fever. Hasn't anyone ever done that to you before?" she asked.

He shook his head while keeping his eyes locked with hers. "No, they usually use a thermometer. It gives a more accurate reading."

She chuckled and pushed on his shoulder. When he didn't budge, she frowned up at him.

"Are you going to let me up?"

"How did I get here?" he asked without answering her.

She sighed. "I carried you."

He chuckled and raised his eyebrows, looking down at her. "Tell me another one."

She rolled her eyes and then shrugged. "Fine, I had help."

Staying where he was, he glanced around the empty room.

"She ran off the moment you woke up," she added.

He smiled. "Sounds like she's the smart one." He watched her eyes narrow.

"Now, will you kindly let me up?" She sounded a little irritated.

"Do I?" he asked, ignoring her question once more. Everything was getting mixed in his head and he found he was having a hard time keeping up with her.

"Do you what?" He could tell she had lost her patience.

"Have a fever?" He leaned closer to her and watched her blue eyes go soft.

"Yes." It came out as a whisper. "I'll send up some hot tea and aspirin."

"Thank you, Sarah." Then something clicked in his memory. This was the employee he was sent up here to evaluate. This was the woman who was applying for the management position at East Haven Resort.

He rolled over quickly, letting her take her escape as he looked up at the ceiling.

When he heard his door click shut, he closed his eyes as he tried to settle his mind and forget the soft body that had been under his just a moment ago.

A few minutes later, there was a light knock at his door. Instantly, he got his hopes up about seeing the blonde once more.

But when he opened the door, he frowned down at an attractive redhead instead. She was carrying a large tray with soup, tea, and a bottle of aspirin.

"I'm Lilith." She smiled. "If there's anything you need while you're here, just let me know."

"Thanks for helping Sarah carry me up here," he

guessed, leaning against the door as she set his tray down on the table across from his bed.

"Oh!" she said as she almost tipped the tray over. When she looked over at him, he could see a blush spread across her cheeks. "We weren't sure—"

"I'm sure the soup and tea will help my cold," he interrupted.

She nodded, looking relieved not to have to explain further. "I have your stuff." She rushed out the door and came back with his overnight bag. "How long will you be staying with us?" she asked, meeting his eyes.

"Until my job is done." He smiled and held the door open for her. She nodded and walked out without any more questions.

He didn't like tipping off the staff when he evaluated one of their own. Especially since he guessed that the two ladies were close friends.

He couldn't afford for Sarah Holley to know that she was being interviewed for one of the highest-paying jobs with Elite Resorts International.

Sarah rushed out of the room and leaned back on the closed door. She covered her heart with a hand and felt her heart almost jump out of her chest. What on earth was that? She closed her eyes and took a few deep breaths to try and steady herself.

She knew what attraction was, but this was a step above anything she'd ever felt. Hard. Fast. Mind-blowing.

Finally, when her heart settled, she went down the narrow steps. At the bottom, she almost knocked over

Lilith, who was carrying a dark overnight bag up the stairs.

"Here, you deal with this." Her friend shoved the bag towards her.

"Oh no. Not after that disappearing act, you just pulled on me. You take it to him. He's awake." She pushed the bag back into Lilith's hands and rushed past her. "While you're at it, take him some hot tea and aspirin," she said over her shoulder just before closing the back door behind her.

When the cool night air hit her face, she felt a little steadier. She could hear the guests out front on the porch, enjoying their last night on the island. She set off from the doorway to walk in the opposite direction.

She would be leaving herself in a couple nights to head home for a few days off. She enjoyed staying on the island, but she also liked her private time. Especially since it appeared that Elite Resorts had hired another man to do her job.

Deciding she could use a short walk to cool off, she turned to the left and hit the small pathway that led to the swimming beach. The pebbles crunched under her feet as she walked in the darkness. The air was cool enough that she rolled down the sleeves on her shirt for the extra warmth. Soon the nights would be warm enough that she could enjoy a swim from the beach, but tonight she knew the water was way too cold.

Stopping a few feet away from the shoreline, she sat in the soft sand and pulled her knees up to her chest. Her thoughts turned towards Benjamin Rothschild's body next to hers.

She'd had her share of lovers. Nothing to brag about,

but enough that she'd learned to never hold back when she felt attraction. Mutual attraction. And one thing was clear after the incident upstairs: Mr. Rothschild had been mutually attracted.

She couldn't afford to have an affair with the man who had the potential to be her new boss. Even if he was sex in a suit, with dark mysterious eyes which called to her and promised long lazy nights of pleasure.

Sighing, she closed her eyes and thought that if she were her mother, she'd have no problem taking the man to bed. Chuckling a little, she glanced over towards the mainland. It was just far enough that she couldn't see lights through the vast darkness.

Her mother was her own special breed, a true child of the hippy movement who'd never really grown out of it. Crystal Holley was… unique. In every sense.

She loved her mother more than anyone else on earth. And she was proud of her for being who she was and not falling victim to the preppy world that had surrounded Silver Cove since her childhood.

Resting back on her elbows, she glanced up at the stars, her eyes moving to where Venus should be. The memory of her father popped into her head like it always did when she looked at the stars.

He'd held her on this very beach, pointing at the stars as he told her the story of Venus and the other planets and constellations.

The first and only man she'd ever loved had been taken from her life too quickly. Cancer had caused her hero to shrivel and melt right before her six-year-old eyes. Her mother had never been the same after his death. Even for a woman who chose to walk her own path, she'd gone a little off the edge after her true love's death.

It was one of the main reasons Sarah had stayed around Silver Cove instead of heading out into the world like her friends had after graduating. That, and East Haven Resort.

Sarah turned her head and smiled at the lights from the main building. This place was home more than the two-story Victorian house, which sat on the corner of Main and First in downtown Silver Cove. The Victorian had been in her mother's family for generations. Looking back at the lit building behind her, the resort that had been her father's, she wondered if that part of her heritage would ever be under her control. As it should be.

Standing up, she dusted the sand from her skirt and started making her way back towards the lights and sounds. When she entered the back kitchen, Lilith and Adam, her newly hired chef, were arguing once again.

"What is it this time?" she hissed as she shut the door to the kitchen behind her. The two of them turned and glared at her. She didn't know where the guests had gone to, but she couldn't chance them hearing the pair.

"This man wants to send this"—she waved at a bowl full of dark liquid— "nasty smelling stuff up to what could be our new boss." Lilith crossed her arms over her chest. The smell instantly hit Sarah, almost causing her to take a few steps back.

"What is that?" she asked, wanting to plug her nose.

Adam glanced at her and shrugged. "An old family recipe that is guaranteed to have Mr. Rothschild back on his feet by morning." The man's heavy French accent did little to reassure her.

"What's in it?" she asked, moving a little closer.

"You can't be seriously thinking of giving this to someone." Lilith glared at her and then turned her burning eyes back to Adam.

"Maybe. My mother used to give me something like that." She nodded to the brown mixture. Taking another smell, she realized the strongest odor was from the onions. "It looks like a mix of onion soup and… is that honey?"

"Oui." Adam nodded his head and smiled. "Brown sugar, honey, onions, and… secret family spices."

She dipped her finger into the mix and tasted. "It's better than it smells." She turned to Lilith. "It couldn't hurt."

Lilith shook her head. "I won't take it to him. I took up the soup and this..." She shivered. "You'll have to do it yourself."

Sarah frowned. She'd hoped to avoid the man for as long as she could. At least until she could come up with a more permanent plan for staying out of his way or getting him fired.

"Fine." She thought about it. If Adam's concoction actually worked, maybe she'd get some credit. If it didn't… well, she'd think about that later. "I'll take it up then." She picked up the tray, pushed open the kitchen door, and started up the narrow steps. When she knocked on the door, she held her breath as she heard him moving around the room.

When he answered, with nothing more than a white towel hanging low on his hips, her breath hitched, and she felt her face flush. Desire spread through her so fast, she wondered that the soup she was holding didn't begin to boil.

He was a lot taller and broader chested than she'd first

thought. No wonder they'd had a hard time carrying him; he was packed with muscles. Lean, sexy muscles covered in tight, tan skin with a light dusting of hair over his chest, which made her want to reach out and run her fingers over every inch of him. Her mouth watered at the thought of taking her time exploring him.

She heard him chuckle and her eyes moved up to his face. His nose was red like it had been blown one too many times, and she could tell he was at a point of exhaustion by the redness in his eyes.

Shaking the thoughts of pleasure from her mind, she cleared her throat.

"Our chef wants me to give you his family's secret recipe to help with your cold." She started pushing the tray towards him, but he didn't move.

Instead, he just smiled and leaned against the door. "Come to finish the job?"

She blinked a few times. "Pardon?"

He chuckled and glanced down at her. When he didn't say anything more, she felt her face flush further.

"I hope you didn't think…" She broke off, appalled that she was acting like a schoolgirl. "Mr. Rothschild, I am a professional. We were simply trying to get you into your room before any of our current guests could see you incapacitated."

He looked at her for a moment and nodded, and then he stood back for her to enter the room.

"The soup, tea, and hot shower have done wonders already," he said as she set the tray down next to his empty dishes. To keep herself busy, she gathered them up and piled them on the tray to take with her. When she turned, she almost bumped solidly into his chest.

"I hope that tastes better than it smells." He frowned down at the steaming bowl.

"It does. My mother used to give me something close to it. Chef Carriveau assures me that you'll be back on your feet by morning."

He glanced down at his feet and then looked up at her. She watched as a slow smile spread on his lips until she had a view of his perfect white teeth. Dressed only in a white towel, with his dark hair wet and pushed away from his still unshaven face, the smile made him look downright dangerous. Even if he was sick as a dog, the man dripped with sexuality.

"Looks like I'm halfway there already."

"Well, drink it or not, it's up to you." She moved to walk around him, but he stopped her by putting a hand on her arm.

"Are you always this concerned about the health of your guests?"

"We both know you're not our standard guest."

He sighed and nodded, and she watched a weary look cross his eyes. "How did you know?"

She shrugged. "It became obvious when you paid for the reservations with an ERI business card." She moved to go around him once more. When he stopped her again, she glared up at him. "How long will you be staying here?" she asked as she tried to keep her voice level.

He shrugged his shoulders and she felt her frustration grow.

"If that's all tonight, Mr. Rothschild, I'd like to check on the other guests before turning in myself."

"This isn't going to be a problem, is it?" he asked, stopping her from moving around him once more.

"This?" She nodded between them. When he smiled, she frowned. "There is no *this*." She raised her chin a little then quickly ducked around him. She felt pleased with herself until she heard him chuckle behind her. She stopped at the door, balancing the tray in one hand and holding onto the door handle with another, as she glanced over her shoulder.

"What?" She frowned a little and tried to ignore how sexy he looked with the light behind him, glowing over all that beautiful skin.

"Mark my words. There is a *this*." He waved his hand between them.

Without responding to him, she turned and fled the room as she tried to think of a way to get Benjamin Rothschild out of her domain as quickly as possible.

CHAPTER 3

By the next morning, Benjamin was feeling almost one hundred percent again. Well enough to enjoy a light jog around the island. He had to admit, the place was beautiful.

East Haven Resort sat on the very tip of its own private island, which boasted a small golf course, three swimming pools, a private sandy beach, spa accommodations to rival the best hotels, and a large garden area equipped with many ponds and gazebos for those special events. Everything the wealthy would need for a getaway.

But the icing on the cake was the huge white four-story building itself. Looking at it was like stepping back in time. It had clean white siding and a bright red roof with flags at each peak. There were a few large stone chimneys that rose up in different places on the large building.

On the main level, large white columns held up the second and third story secluded deck areas, which were split into smaller spaces off of each private room.

Deep green lawns surrounded the building and long wide steps leading up to the main level veranda, which could easily accommodate a party of fifty. Tables and chairs lined a whole side of the building that overlooked the largest of the three swimming pools.

If you made your way around towards the ocean side, the tables and chairs were replaced with porch swings and recliners for guests to lazily enjoy the beautiful views of the water. There was a smaller pool here with a hot tub on each end for guests to relax and watch the evening stars pass overhead.

Making your way even further around the wraparound porch, the next side overlooked the private garden areas. There were secluded trails that wound their way through the endless flowers and bushes towards the golf course and tennis courts area where there was also another swimming pool.

Finally, on the very back of the large building, there was a more private area set aside for the staff entrances and a small sitting area, no doubt used for staff meals and smoke breaks.

His room was on the third floor. He guessed that the staff was housed in the older two-story building that sat just off the parking lot and dock areas. He had a perfect view of it out of his window.

Still, his room was more than adequate. Actually, the sheer size of the room was quite intimidating. He'd first imagined that Sarah had put him up in one of the larger guest rooms. But when the early morning sun had streaked through his curtains, he'd gotten a glance of the view and realized otherwise.

Still, the room was overly large. Everything seemed perfect, from the extra high shine in the dark oak flooring to the intricate crown molding on the ceilings. Even the large bathroom had gleamed with beauty. The crisp white tiles and oversized claw tub/shower combo had been a pleasure to enjoy last night when he'd felt bad.

Nothing was out of place in his rooms. Every aspect of the place was made to please the eye and make the occupants feel at home.

That perfection had flowed outside his rooms as well. He'd walked through the corridors expecting… well, he didn't know what. He only knew that he'd never experienced anything like it before.

His eyes took in everything as he'd jogged around the private island, and he'd made mental notes of places he wanted to visit again. He'd taken a little longer on his run than normal since he'd stopped a half-dozen times to just enjoy the view.

When he finally headed back up to his room, he showered and dressed quickly. Then he headed down the long three-story spiral staircase and walked into the dining room that sat to the left of the front doors. There were two other couples enjoying breakfast already and he stopped to chat with them for a moment before finally taking his seat next to the fireplace. Its warmth spread throughout him quickly, making him realize he might have overdone it on the run that morning.

"How are you this morning, Mr. Rothschild?" He looked up to see Lilith smiling down at him. She was wearing a simple black skirt and a white apron over her cream blouse.

"Much better today." He smiled up at her as she handed him a menu.

"The chef's daily specials are listed on the front. Can I get you a cup of coffee?"

"No, but I'll have some tea with honey." He set the menu down and glanced around. "Is Miss Holley around this morning?"

"She's welcoming our new guests," Lilith said, nodding towards the front of the building. "I'll go get your tea." He glanced out the large windows and saw Sarah with a handful of people on the lawn. She appeared to be showing them around the grounds, so he turned his attention back to the menu.

There were too many wonderful things listed for him to make a choice. When Lilith walked over with his tea, he asked her for her favorite dish.

"My favorite is the crepes with salted butter and caramel. But, I'm a caramel lover. If you like fruit better, you can't go wrong with the chef's Belgian waffles. They're topped with the best fruit sauce and fresh fruit. If you're a health nut, the eggs and black truffles with vegetables are good."

He chuckled when she made a funny face. "You don't go for the healthy stuff often?"

She shook her head. "Not for breakfast. I always have a salad for lunch and dinner, but... breakfast is where the fun food is." She smiled, and he could tell he was going to like the woman.

"Then the crepes it is." He handed her the menu.

"Perfect choice." She nodded and disappeared.

He turned his attention back to the window, but the

group had moved out of range. Pulling out his phone, he checked his email while he waited for his food.

There was a pretty lengthy email from his boss, explaining his opinions and the questions he wanted to be answered about Sarah. He was scrolling through the list when he felt a shadow fall over his table.

"I see you're feeling better." Sarah stood beside his table. She was dressed in a cream suit today. A light crease ran down the front of both of her pant legs, and low heels clicked on the floor as she moved closer. The matching jacket was a light material and he could see a low cut blouse tucked underneath.

Her long blonde hair was pulled back and held tightly at the nape of her neck. He missed seeing it fall around her face in ringlets.

Last night she hadn't been wearing any jewelry, except for the diamonds in her ears, but today, they were replaced by small gold hoops. There was a gold chain that hung between her breasts, causing him to remember how nice they had felt against his chest last night. When she flipped a curl of her hair away from her eyes, gold chains and bracelets clattered together. He noticed she was wearing several rings on her fingers and wondered if the one on her ring finger was a band of significance.

"Yes, much better. You can thank the chef for the broth. It seemed to help."

She nodded. "I'm sure you'll want to meet with the staff soon." She gripped her hands together. "It's a pretty busy morning, but we can make time in about an hour?"

He nodded slightly and marveled at the difference the sunlight made on her. Today she was all business. From the way she held herself to how she dressed. But he remembered all too well that last night she'd been a sexy gypsy goddess.

"Do you have an office?" he asked, just as Lilith started across the room with his tray of food.

Sarah nodded briskly. "It's on the fourth floor at the end of the hallway." She smiled slightly at Lilith and then stepped out of the way. "We'll see you in an hour."

He watched Sarah move across the floor quickly and then looked down. His mouth watered as Lilith set the plate of food before him, and he realized that for the first time in days, he was starving.

Sarah rushed up the back stairs, taking two steps at a time. When she pushed into her office—what would soon be his office—she closed the door and took a couple deep breaths. Why was this happening now? And more important, why did he have to look so much better looking this morning?

He'd shaved the dark stubble from his face, which had been extra sexy on him last night. She'd thought he would have a baby face once cleaned, but somehow, he looked even more dangerous than before. His dark eyes had danced over her, making her body very aware of what she wanted him to do to her. Even her nipples had puckered when his gaze had roamed over them. Betrayal. Her body knew what it wanted even if her mind kept telling her to back off.

There was no time for her to explore anything further with him. Especially since she wasn't quite clear on what he was doing here in the first place. After inquiring, the memo she'd received in reply from ERI had been vague at best. The man was down here to do an evaluation. What or whom he was evaluating had been left unanswered, but Sarah had worked it out on her own. It was an evaluation period, to see if the man wanted the job. She'd heard his name over the last few years. It appeared that Mr. Rothschild had been on a steady climb to the top of the very private company.

For six months, she'd been left to run East Haven all by herself. The books showed a profit since Tom Elliott, the last general manager, had retired.

Tom had been the manager of East Haven for as long as she could remember, even before her father passed away. Tom had been the one who had taken a chance on her and hired her at the tender age of fifteen.

Sarah had needed to get out of working in her mother's store, Serenity's Attic. She needed to know that she could be much more than what she was. Instead of using her birth name on the application, she'd put a much more sophisticated one. That day she'd become Sarah Holley, an employee at East Haven Resorts, instead of Serenity Sunshine Holley, daughter of the local hippie store's owner.

For the first couple years, Sarah had spent her time cleaning rooms, shuttling back and forth from the mainland each day. Then, shortly after graduation, Tom had given her a raise and a room in the back building where all the other week-on, week-off employees stayed.

Glancing around the small office space that she'd made her own in the past few months, she realized just how much she'd miss doing what she did now. She'd been born for the job. Chuckling, she realized just how true that statement was.

She sat behind her desk and laid her head down on the solid wood. So much had changed over the last few months that she just couldn't imagine taking a step backward and returning to her mundane life of answering to yet another manager.

She tried to keep her mind occupied for the next forty-five minutes. But the fact was, with every tick of the clock, she knew her future was closing in on her.

Finally, there was a light knock on her door and she felt her heart skip several beats. When Lilith pushed it open, she released the breath she'd been holding.

"Is he here yet?" Her friend peeked her head in the doorway.

"No, come in," she whispered and waved her in. "Tell me everything is going to work out," she said as her friend sat in the chair on the other side of the desk.

"Of course, it is." She waved her hand and Sarah could tell it was a lie. "After all, he seems like a very nice man." Just then there was another knock and they both looked at one another.

"Come in," Sarah called out. Once again, she relaxed when she saw Adam stroll in.

"Am I late?" he asked, frowning down at Lilith.

"No, just on time," she said, waving him in. Shortly after, Rodney, the groundskeeper, Carmen, the head of housekeeping, and Heather, the events director, all piled into her small office. There were numerous employees under each of her head staff, but for this meeting, she'd only called them in.

"Thank you, everyone, for coming. I'm sure Mr. Rothschild will want to meet with each and every one of you in the upcoming days." She watched as nervous looks were exchanged. "Remember, we all represent ERI's best interest and as such—" She was interrupted by another knock on the door. Rodney opened it and stood back as Benjamin walked into the small space.

Just his presence made the room feel smaller. His eyes moved around as she introduced him to each head staff member.

"All in all, there are twenty-four full-time employees. Twenty-five including myself." She nodded to him, showing that he now had the floor.

"Um…" He cleared his throat. "It's a pleasure to meet everyone. I'm looking forward to having a chance to talk with each of you one-on-one over the next few days." He nodded. "Now, please…" He motioned towards the door. "I know how busy your days must be."

He stood back as the room cleared. Lilith glanced at Sarah over her shoulder as she walked out the door.

She watched Benjamin shut the door behind the last employee and then turn towards her. "Now, if you don't mind, I'd like to start with you." He walked over and took the chair opposite her.

She leaned forward and tried to hide her nerves. She hated being interviewed for jobs. And this felt like an interview.

"What would you like to know?"

His smile was quick, and he glanced down at her hands, which she'd gripped together on the desk.

"For starters. Are any of those by chance wedding or engagement rings?" He leaned his elbows on his knees and looked at her, waiting.

Tilting her chin up, she decided the best way to handle her new potential boss was to lead him in the direction she wanted.

"I have a list of the staff on hand." She opened her file and handed over the sheet of paper, which he didn't take, so she set it in front of him. "Here are the budget reports along with profit and…"

"Are you going to ignore my question?" he broke in.

She sighed and tried to keep her anger in check. "Mr. Rothschild, my job is to make your job easier. I fail to see how my personal life has anything to do with that task."

"Humor me." His voice was low and for some reason, touched her more than his sexy smile did.

Not speaking, she shook her head slightly.

"No, what?" he asked.

"No, they are just rings."

The left side of his mouth tipped up in a sexy grin that sent quick pulses throughout her entire body.

"You?" she asked, moving her hands under her desk.

He shook his head from side to side. "Have you always lived in Silver Cove?"

"Yes. You're from Boston?" When he nodded, she asked. "Always?" He nodded again, giving her that sexy grin once more.

"Ever been married?" he asked, looking quite comfortable in the small chair.

She shook her head, no. "You?" He did the same.

"Where did you go to school?" he asked. This time, she blinked and felt her shoulders tense. Taking a few cleansing breaths, she glanced down at the folder in front of her.

"My references are…" She started to push the folder towards him.

"I know everything that's in there. I'm asking about grade school, high school. Was it local or were you home-schooled?"

"I was homeschooled for a few years until my knowledge outgrew my mother's. Then I demanded to go to public school until graduation. You?" She leaned back in her chair, trying to release the stress that always came with answering to her lack of education.

"Private schools until I was shipped off to Harvard."

She felt herself tense even further. If anything could persuade her that an affair with the man sitting across from her wasn't a good idea, just hearing the word *Harvard* had.

"If you don't mind, I'd like to get back to business." She pushed the folder across the table at him and watched him frown.

"Why?" He ignored the folder altogether. "I thought we had something"—he waved between them— "going here."

Blinking several times, she leaned forward again. "I've tried having… something… with a coworker before. It doesn't work out. Actually, it tends to just mess everything up."

She watched him tilt his head. "Did he break your heart?"

She felt like laughing. The man was on a one-way track. "No, I broke things off." She turned to her computer. "We have a large party in a few hours which I will need to help set up, so if we're done…" She looked over at him.

He leaned back and crossed his arms over his chest.

"I'm well aware of the schedule around here. I do have a few more questions."

She turned towards him. "Shoot."

"When you're not living here, where do you stay?"

"With my mother in Silver Cove."

"What does your mother do?"

She felt her shoulders tense once more and braced herself for what she knew would come next.

CHAPTER 4

*B*en waited for her answer as he watched a rainbow of emotions cross Sarah's face. Finally, her eyes turned sad as her lips tilted up in a sexy smile.

"She runs her own business," she said briskly.

"What type of business?" He was curious. The file on Sarah had been pretty extensive, except when it came to her personal life.

She shrugged and turned back to her computer. "It's like a general store."

"Like?" He leaned on his knees once more. He could tell she was hiding something, and he wanted to know why.

"She sells organic groceries, local wares, and… other things."

His eyebrows shot up. He wondered why she was so hesitant to talk about it. From the sound of it, she should be proud that her mother was making her own way.

"I'd like to meet her. I'm a huge shopper at the organic farmer's markets downtown."

She chuckled and shook her head. "I'm sure you'd get a kick out of it." She turned back to him. "Any other questions?"

He thought about it. "Do you have dinner plans?"

She blinked and gave him a deer in the headlights look. He couldn't stop himself from smiling. He had a feeling she wasn't easily thrown off, and something inside him marveled at the fact that he could do that to her.

"I'll be helping out with the dinner party." It was nothing more than a whisper.

"How about after? What do you say to meeting me on the swim beach for some dessert?"

She drawled, "Did you actually think that line would work?"

Instead of answering, he continued, "I hear the chef makes a killer chocolate mousse. I'm sure the French man wouldn't mind if we snuck some away from the party." He wiggled his eyebrows and gave her one of his killer smiles that had always caused the women to fall right into his hands.

She sighed, and he could tell he'd hit a weak spot. He wasn't sure if it was his smile or the promise of the chocolate. She closed her eyes and he could see that she was wrestling with the decision.

"We can call it a professional meeting if it makes you feel better," he added.

Finally, she said, "You bring the dessert." Her eyes met his. "Strictly professional."

He nodded and got up quickly. He knew to make a quick retreat before she had a chance to change her mind.

"I'll see you at eight?" he said, and she nodded as he let himself out of the small office.

Ben spent the next few hours asking as many questions as he could without getting in the way.

He'd enjoyed a wonderful lunch out on the front porch with a few other new guests and then took a long walk around the grounds. He had a nice chat with Rodney, the head groundskeeper, who couldn't stop saying nice things about Sarah and how she'd stepped up after the last manager had retired.

The man was old enough to be a great-grandfather and, in Ben's opinion, was a decade behind retirement. Yet after spending half an hour trying to keep up with the man while he worked, Ben changed his mind. The job was clearly what Rodney lived for.

It didn't take him long to figure out that most of it was thanks to Sarah and her management skills. The woman was a natural at organization.

By the time the dinner party had started, he had to admit, the place ran very smoothly.

After the sun had sunk below the trees, he made his way to the kitchen, where Adam had packed a small container that he had arranged earlier. He'd tucked an extra blanket from his room under his arm and carried the entire thing to the beach.

When he arrived, Sarah was already there, standing knee deep in the water. She'd changed into another long flowing skirt, and this time, had on a knit sweater, which was almost see-through. He watched her turn towards him. The full moon was behind her, shimmering low over the water. Her hair was loose from its clips, flowing past her shoulders. She looked like she'd just walked out of the dark water and belonged in the forest that surrounded the small clearing.

Sarah watched Benjamin walk towards her and felt her heart skip a few beats. He'd changed out of the dress pants, shirt, and tie from earlier. Now he wore a well-worn pair of jeans and a dark sweater, which made him look like he belonged on the cover of a magazine.

She'd seen him walking the grounds and talking with her staff, which had only heightened her nerves and anger about the possibility of him taking her job. Still, she felt an undeniable pull towards him that she needed to explore.

"Isn't that water freezing?" he asked, stopping a few feet away from her.

She glanced down at her feet and shook her head. "It's a nice reprieve from the heels I was wearing earlier." She walked out of the crisp water, her feet feeling immensely better than when she'd removed the shoes she'd run around in all day.

She stood back and watched him set down a large basket and then spread a blanket over the sand.

"So, how was your chat with Rodney?" she asked nervously as she fidgeted with the hem of her sweater.

He glanced up at her, his dark eyebrows shooting up.

"The groundskeeper." He nodded.

"Good." He looked back down, focused on arranging the food on the edge of the blanket.

She took a few steps forward. "I know he's older, but in the entire time I've worked here, I've never seen the man slow down. He loves his job. Loves this place." She glanced around the pristine beach, knowing that he raked the sand at least twice a week. More often, during the busy season.

Benjamin glanced up and nodded. "I don't doubt it." He smiled as he patted the spot next to him on the blanket.

"Well?" she asked, putting her hands on her hips and glaring down at him.

"Well, what?" He looked up at her.

She felt like groaning. "Are you going to let him stay on or not?" she asked between clenched teeth.

"Why does it matter to you?"

She took another step towards him. "Rodney has been on this island since before our parents were born. This is where he wants to be." She glanced around again and could see every detail he'd worked his entire life for. "If you're just going to come here"—she put her hands back on her hips and moved closer— "and upset all the employees by deciding who stays and who goes…"

His chuckle stopped her, causing her chin to drop a little as she looked down at him.

"Are you going to stand here lecturing me on how to do my job all evening? Or can we set it all aside and enjoy the moon and some really good food?"

She crossed her arms over her chest and stood her ground.

He sighed and said, "Rodney isn't going anywhere." He patted the spot next to him. "Better? Now can we enjoy this spread?"

She looked into his dark eyes and could see he was telling her the truth. She walked over slowly and sat next to him. Tucking her long skirt around her feet underneath her, she got comfortable. "Did Adam give you a hard time?"

"No. Actually, everyone seems to be very cooperative." He handed her a cup of chocolate mousse topped with fresh strawberries. "I have a feeling you had something to do with that."

She took a spoonful and closed her eyes as she tasted the richness on the tip of her tongue.

"This is better than sex," she moaned as she scooped up another spoonful. Realizing he'd stopped moving and breathing, she glanced over at him. "Relax." She chuckled. "Try some. You'll probably agree." She leaned back on her elbows and glanced up at the clear night.

He seemed to come out of the trance and started scooping his own spoon into his mouth. "I'd have to say a close second." He mimicked her relaxed posture. His knee brushed up against hers and she felt a zing of awareness rush up her legs.

"Tell me about your meetings today," she said, wanting to keep the conversation off of the growing spark between them.

Chuckling, he scooped another spoonful into his mouth and shook his head. "I'd rather talk about this."

When she didn't answer him, he set his cup aside, and then took hers and set it next to his. When he reached up and brushed a strand of her curly hair away from her face, she held her breath. "Whether we want to admit it or not, there's this pull." He used his fingertips to raise her chin up until she looked into his dark eyes. "Something I have no intention of fighting." It was a whisper just above her lips.

He paused, giving her time to pull away. But again, her

body betrayed her by leaning in and closing the distance before she had time to think all the way through her actions.

When their lips met, a quick zing rushed through her body, a better high than the chocolate mousse on her tongue had given her moments ago.

Her hands moved into his hair automatically, pulling him closer, holding him hostage to the onslaught her mouth demanded from his. His hair was rich and thick between her fingers as he moved over her, pinning her to the blanket and soft sand below.

His hands gently roamed from her shoulder down to her hips as his tongue played slowly with hers. She couldn't stop the moan from escaping her lips when his mouth traveled down her neck, leaving goose bumps rising over her skin as he went.

When his hand started to move upward, taking her sweater with it, she jerked and pushed him away. "This is crazy," she said, quickly sitting up and pulling her sweater back in place.

"Not as crazy as fighting it," he said, moving beside her. She had to give him credit for not touching her more. She didn't know if she'd be able to stop herself again. Not when her body was running so hot.

She moved to get up, but a hand on her elbow stopped her. "Don't go." His voice was a little rough and she glanced over at him as he cleared his throat. "Stay, enjoy the dessert." He handed her the cup of chocolate again. "Tell me about your childhood." He leaned back, looking quite comfortable. Almost like they hadn't just been moments away from ripping one another's clothes off and having wild sex on the beach.

Trying to steady herself, she took another spoonful of the rich dessert, hoping it would settle her system back down. But the creamy chocolate only heightened her desire for more. Of the dessert and of him.

"Why are you so interested?" She sat up and tucked her knees to her chest as she finished off the cup of mousse.

He chuckled, causing her to glance back at him. "I would have thought that was obvious."

She tilted her head and looked at him. "You know what I mean."

Reaching over, he once again played with her hair, ignoring her question. "Were you raised on the island alongside Rodney?"

She sighed and set her cup aside, then tucked her arms around her legs. Deciding to play along, she tilted her head and answered.

"One of my first memories is here." She glanced around the dark beach and smiled as she remembered the evening family picnics they used to have.

The memory of her father surfaced followed quickly by the last time she could remember seeing the only man she'd ever really loved.

Her eyes unfocused as she looked out over the dark water.

It was a week after her fifth birthday. She'd been very excited to meet her "other" grandparents for the very first time. She'd even dressed up in her fanciest dress, the pink one with yellow flowers. She'd helped her mother comb her hair and tied a yellow ribbon in it, to keep the curls under control.

But her grandparents hadn't seemed excited to meet

her. They had rushed past her and closed themselves up in the dining room with her father. She and her mother waited near the bottom of the stairs as they listened to them argue in the next room.

Finally, when she heard her daddy's voice raise, she broke free from her mother's hold and pushed into the room, rushing straight to her father's side.

"Stop yelling at my daddy!" she'd shouted while stomping her foot at the man, who looked like a much older version of her father. He was a lot rounder than her dad and had a stern look on his face, something she'd never seen on her father's face.

In the last year, her father had gone from taking her hiking and swimming, to lying in bed with machines and tubes hooked into his arms. Even now, he sat in a chair with wheels on it and sucked air from a mask.

When he held her hand, she noticed how thin his skin looked and it made her sad.

"Leave us be, child," her grandfather had barked.

"Serenity..." Her father looked down at her and brushed away her tear with his thin fingers. "Be a good girl and go back out with your mama. I promise we're almost done here."

She heard someone huff and glanced over at the woman, who had crossed her arms over her ample chest. "What kind of name is that for our grandchild?"

She crossed her arms over her own chest and frowned at the woman. "I don't like them here. In our house, Papa." She frowned over to the couple sitting across from her dad.

There were several other people in the room, but none

of them mattered. Not when she knew it was the older couple that had upset her daddy.

"Be a good girl now." He nodded behind her and suddenly her mother was there, holding her, carrying her from the room.

"Don't let them yell at you, Daddy," she called back as she tried to break free from her mother's hold. Tears streamed down her face.

When her mother set her down on her bed, she tucked her body around Snuffy, her stuffed elephant, and looked up at her mother.

"Why are they here anyway?" she asked between sobs.

"Daddy sent for them, remember? He's sick and he wants to make sure we have what we need after he's gone."

"I don't want daddy to go!" She kicked her little legs and crossed her arms over her chest again.

"We've talked about this," her mother said, leaning closer and pushing a strand of her strawberry hair behind her ear. "Daddy has to go to the stars. It's his time soon. Just like one day, all of us will take the long journey."

"I don't want to!" She kicked again. Her mother picked her up and held her close.

Her little mind swirled around what her mother had told her. "Can I keep Snuffy?" she asked, wiping the tears from her eyes.

"Yes, of course, you can."

"Where will we live without daddy?" she asked, looking around her room. Already her mother had been packing her stuff into boxes.

"I told you. We're going to go live with Granny and

Papa." She smiled, brushing a hand over her hair. "In the big house on the mainland."

"I don't want to!" She kicked again, this time using less energy since her head was feeling heavy. "What's going to happen to here?"

Her mother looked around the room, rocking her slowly. "I don't know, sweetie, but from the sounds of the meeting, it might not be part of your heritage anymore."

Sarah's mind returned to the present when Ben's hand rested on her shoulder.

"Where did you just go?" His voice was soft, next to her ear.

"My father died when I was six. He had colon cancer." She used the sleeve of her sweater to wipe away the tears before he would notice them. "We used to spend a lot of time on this beach, watching the stars pass above." She glanced up and felt her heart skip.

"I'm sorry," he said, wrapping his arm around her.

She leaned back and looked over at him. "Up until that year, I had been raised at East Haven, as if it were my home." She sighed and looked back over the water as Ben pulled her closer and she rested her head against him. "In fact, I still think of it that way." She paused, then pulled out of his arms and stood up. "And nothing or no one is ever going to change that." She waited until his eyes met hers. "Thank you for the pudding and… everything." His mouth opened quickly and then closed again, and she turned around and picked up her shoes and walked back to the employee's building.

y the next day, Ben was beginning to wonder why ERI hadn't given Sarah the job as general manager years ago. From the sounds of it, she'd been in that position even before Tom Elliott had retired. Every last employee that he'd interviewed said they loved her and talked about how much she'd done for the resort.

When he stepped out on the front deck to make a private call, he was surprised to see a lone guest standing near the railing, looking out over the water. He almost turned around to walk back inside, when he heard the woman sniffle.

"Is everything okay?" he asked, taking a step closer.

When the young attractive woman in her early twenties turned around, he thought he saw a slight curve play on her lips.

"Oh, yes." She started to turn around but stopped. "It's just hard getting over Ken." She sighed and leaned against the post, crossing her arms slightly over her ample chest.

"I'll leave…" he started to say, but she interrupted him.

"Oh, no. Please. I rather think I'd enjoy a distraction from my sorrows." She patted the railing next to her.

Something in his mind screamed for him to walk away, but he didn't want to be rude to a guest. Not when he could see a few people watching from inside the dining hall.

He walked over and stopped right next to her. He noticed that her eyes were red from crying and instantly felt bad for questioning her motives in the first place.

"Are you here with the new group?" He nodded towards the large glass window where a small group of people was eating breakfast. He noticed Lilith glancing at him occasionally as she served everyone their breakfasts.

"Yes, it's Mary's birthday. Her family has been coming here since she was sixteen." The woman sighed and her eyes zeroed in on a pretty brunette who was sitting at the head of the table. "You would think that her parents would realize that this place is dull. I mean, just last week she was telling us that we were going to spend her birthday weekend in New York." The woman sighed again and turned around to gaze out at the water. "There's not much to do up here except watch the waves and grow old."

He chuckled. "I take it you like a faster pace?"

She turned to him. "Doesn't everyone?"

He thought about it and shrugged. "I've only ever known city life."

She smiled. "It must be wonderful. New York that is."

He chuckled. "It has its moments. Have you ever been?"

"No, but I've been to Boston plenty of times." She pouted slightly, making him wonder if she was younger than he'd first thought. He leaned against the post and nodded to the dining room.

"How old is Mary turning?"

"Nineteen." She glanced towards the window and put her arm through his. "Why don't you take me for a walk? I hear there's a garden somewhere a person could get lost in."

He tried to hold in a chuckle. "I wish I could, but I've got work to do. Actually," he continued when he noticed she was about to pout and try to talk him into it, "I only came out here because I needed to make a phone call to my boss." He wiggled his phone in his hand. "The garden is just around there." He pointed. "You'll enjoy the flowers and the fresh air will help you get over your man."

She dropped her arm from his and stormed back into the dining room without another word. He watched her go and realized he hadn't even asked her name.

Turning on his phone, he pushed off from the railing and started walking in the direction of the gardens to make his call. He figured if the young blonde wasn't going to enjoy them, he might as well.

"Yeah? It's about time you called," Carl Harrison barked back at him through the phone.

"I didn't know you were expecting daily updates." He smiled as he ducked under a low branch on a tree. The leaves had yet to show themselves completely for spring, but there were enough to know that in a few weeks, the entire place would be green.

"What's the scoop?" The older man ignored his response.

"Well, after fighting off the flu, I've settled in and made my assessment. I can have…"

"Hold on there," Carl broke in. "How can you know? You've only been up there two days."

Ben held in a groan. He knew where the old man's thinking was going to lead him. "Two days is all I needed to assess—"

"Why don't you give me a call back at the end of the week. Then we can talk."

"Because I don't need until—"

"I sent you up there on a mission. A pretty damn important one. I expect someone of your caliber, who wants to remain in the position you're in, to weigh all the pros and cons before making a decision."

He felt a pang of guilt and knew that it was more than his reputation on the line.

"I'll see you back at the office next Monday."

"I thought you'd say that." Carl laughed. "Now, tell me about the girl." He could hear something in the man's voice but couldn't quite pin it down.

Walking over to a stone bench, he sat down and proceeded to tell his boss about Sarah.

Sarah had sweat rolling down the back of her new white silk blouse and cursed the early warm weather. She had hoped for a few more weeks of the crisp eastern breeze that usually floated in off the water until late May. But here it was only the seventh of the month and it was over seventy degrees out.

Glancing down at the large heavy vase of flowers in her hands, she questioned if they would wilt in the next two hours and if she should have let Lilith and Heather carry them out with the rest of the decorations for the birthday dinner.

She was just rounding the corner on her way to the gazebo area when she heard her name. Stopping in her tracks, she listened closely as a deep voice carried from behind a large hedge.

"There isn't much more I can tell you about Sarah. She seems very competent. She's more than proficient in handling the staff here and everyone seems to not only enjoy her company but respect her. Which is saying something for someone so young."

She shifted the weight of the flowers and crept slowly towards the bush. When Ben stopped talking, she held her breath in hopes of catching a hint at who he was speaking with. She leaned towards the green leaves of the tall bush and wished there was a slight break in the thick leaves so she could at least see him.

"Yes, I understand we're the same age." Ben chuckled. "But..." He was silent again. "Yes, I know..." Another break, so she leaned even further into the bush. "I haven't made up my mind completely, but..." She heard him sigh and could tell he was losing his patience. "Yes, I'll have my report on your desk by next Monday."

She heard him click off his phone and was wondering how she was going to escape without him hearing her when another voice broke in. This one was softer and laced with sex.

"Well, hello. It looks like you wanted to join me after all." Sarah felt her breath freeze up when she heard the woman move closer towards Ben. "And here I thought this weekend was going to be boring."

She didn't wait anymore, but turned and stormed off towards the gazebo, not caring if the couple heard her footsteps or not. When she reached the pavilion, she slammed down the heavy vase of flowers and almost tipped them over, catching them just in time. She knew that Heather and Lilith were close behind her, but she desperately needed some alone time before they started decorating the small gazebo for the dinner party in a few hours.

Pushing off from the tables, she made her way towards the sandy beach at a quick pace. Images of Ben holding a mysterious woman in his arms flashed behind her eyes, causing them to sting by the time she reached the water's edge.

She kicked off her heels when she reached the sand and remembered too late that she was wearing stockings. Bending at the waist, she reached down and rolled the thigh-highs off and tossed them aside. When her toes dipped into the water, she felt steady for the first time that day.

"That was by far the most erotic display I've ever seen on a beach," a deep voice said from somewhere behind her.

She gasped and spun around at the same time a wave pushed her feet out from under her. She lost her footing and fell backward into the cool water.

She must have screamed because when she surfaced again, her mouth was full of salt water and sand. She felt her new blouse cling to her skin and clenched her teeth with anger.

"What did you think you were doing?" she spouted as she pushed her long blonde hair out of her face. Then she heard the laughter and ground her back teeth even more.

"I'm sorry. I didn't know you were going to go jumping in." He rushed towards her, only to be pushed away as she shoved him back a few steps as she moved out of the surf.

"I didn't jump in." She glared at him through her wet hair. "Now I'm soaking wet," she complained as she tossed more wet hair out of her face.

"I can see that." His voice had grown soft and much deeper. His eyes were glued to her shirt and when she glanced down, she realized why. The white silk was solid enough when it was dry, but soaked with salt water, it was now completely see-through, as was her silk bra.

Her eyes quickly moved back to his as she pushed the material away from her skin, which had heated once more under his gaze.

"What are you doing here?" she growled.

"Looking for you." It was nothing more than a whisper, and she realized he was still staring at her chest.

"Eyes up," she snapped, pulling his chin until he looked into her own eyes. His smile was quick and somewhat contagious. "Why were you looking for me? I thought you had a rendezvous in the garden."

"Soooo. That was you." His smile grew, and his arms pulled her closer to him until she could feel her blouse soaking his dry shirt.

She tried to fight him off, so he wouldn't ruin his shirt, but his arms were too strong and she gave up quickly.

"What was me?" she mumbled, not really focusing on the conversation. She'd been overheated when she'd fallen in the cold water but had quickly cooled off in the surf. Now, every drop of water was threatening to turn to steam as she felt his hard body next to hers.

"I thought I heard you in the garden. When…" He stopped and shook his head. "Did you storm off because that girl tried to come on to me?" The side of his lips turned up, and she felt like punching him square in the face.

"No," she growled out. "Of course, not…" She tried to break free again, but he moved again until somehow, they ended up closer than before.

"I'm not the kind of guy that kisses one woman one day and another the next." His breath fell over her face, causing her to still.

"I highly doubt—"

"I wouldn't have pegged you for the jealous type." This time his lips curled up into a full smile as she cursed under her breath. "Or the kind of classy woman who could curse like a sailor."

"I don't curse," she growled out, causing him to laugh.

"Maybe not out loud, but I heard you loud and clear just the same. Like I'm hearing this thought…" His voice dropped, and he moved an inch closer. When his lips brushed over hers, she felt her entire body go lax. His wide hands were at the middle of her back, holding her close without forcing her. She was free to break away at any time if she chose.

Then his tongue darted out and licked the seam of her lips, sending a chill down her legs until she felt her knees go weak. Her fingers dug into his shirt, holding her steady as her mouth moved over his. Her eyes had closed with pleasure when her tongue touched his lightly. She slanted her head, giving him better access so she could enjoy his taste on her lips, her tongue. Her fingers shook as she gripped his shirt, making sure she didn't fall at his feet.

"Sarah," he groaned softly next to her lips. "How could

you think I would want or need anyone else after I've played with you?"

She shook her head slightly, unsure of what he was saying. "I…" She broke off when she heard Heather calling her name from the gazebo area. Dropping her hands, she took a step back. "I have to go." She ran towards the edge of the beach, grabbing up her heels and darting into the trees quickly.

She thought she heard him calling after her, but didn't stop to glance back to see if he was following.

When she made it to the clearing, she quickly made her excuses to Heather and Lilith, telling them that she'd fallen into the surf and needed to go up to her rooms to change before she could help set up for the party.

"Don't worry about it. I'm sure Lilith and I—" Heather started to say.

"No, I'll just be a few minutes." She rushed away, heading back through the garden area. She hoped that she wouldn't run into any guests along the pathway. Unfortunately, she wasn't that lucky.

She had just turned the last corner outside of the main building when she heard a group of women coming towards her. She ducked behind a smaller bush and knelt down to hide until they passed by. She even held her breath, just in case, they could hear her breathing.

When the group got closer, she realized it wasn't necessary since they were talking loudly and giggling.

"Can you believe that's what he said to me?" She heard the same female voice she'd heard when she'd been spying on Ben in the gardens. "And then he ran off like I had the plague."

Sarah heard the woman sniffle and was horrified when

the entire group stopped a few feet away from her hiding spot to comfort her.

"Cara, you know it wasn't your fault about Ken," someone said.

"Yeah, I mean, we all knew Ken was an ass."

She heard a few of the ladies agree in unison.

"Ken was nothing but a lying, cheating—"

"But, I loved him."

"You thought you loved him. If you really did, would you be trying so hard with the sexy god in a suit?"

God in a suit? She closed her eyes and saw an image of Ben walking towards her just a few moments ago on the beach. Yes, he was a sexy god in a suit.

Her taste had never really been for men who dressed so sharply. She had always fallen more for the rugged outdoor type. Maybe it was because no one in town would be caught wearing anything more than worn jeans and flannel shirts. Or maybe because she'd had her fair share of men in sharp suits visit the resort and knew that underneath the beautiful exterior, there was usually a stuck-up child who believed they could get anything or anyone they wanted.

Ben didn't fall into that category, which threw her off.

"He's just a distraction. Really." The woman sighed.

"A sexy as hell distraction that I wouldn't mind playing with," someone else started.

The women had started walking again and their voices dropped off enough that Sarah felt comfortable rushing from behind her hiding spot. She took the stairs up to her room two at a time and dumped her shoes as she shut the door behind her. Peeling off her ruined shirt, she dumped it and her skirt on the floor and flipped on the shower. The warm water did little to clear her mind or make her feel refreshed, so she twisted the knob and allowed cold water to hit her skin for almost a full minute before shutting it off.

Towel drying her hair quickly, she reapplied her makeup and threw on some cream-colored slacks and a warm honey-colored blouse.

Her hair would have to dry on its own since she doubted she had enough time to stand under the blow dryer. Pulling on her heels once more, she rushed from her room and made her way towards the gazebo.

When she arrived, everything for the party was in place and Ben stood up on a short ladder, the sleeves to his shirt rolled up to his elbows as he hung a string of lights on hooks around the gazebo.

Heather and Lilith were busy putting the tablecloths on the small tables and organizing the rest of the flower arrangements.

Her eyes were locked on Ben's back as he reached up and clipped a string of lights.

"God in a suit" kept running over and over in her mind as she walked over to Lilith and helped arrange the place settings.

"What's he doing here?" she whispered to her friend as Ben glanced over his shoulder and winked at her. She could feel his eyes run up and down her crisp dry clothes and felt her face flush with the memory of how he'd looked at her earlier.

Lilith glanced up quickly at Ben, who had turned back around. Her eyes moved back towards Sarah as she shrugged. "He stopped by a few moments after you left," she whispered and leaned closer. "What's going on between you two? And I won't take *nothing* as an answer since I can see how he looks at you." Lilith leaned away just as Ben glanced over his shoulder and glanced at her once more. The heat from his gaze sizzled her skin and caused her cheeks to heat.

She doubted there was any way to hide the fact that there was something between them. "Later," she mouthed just as Ben jumped down from the ladder and started walking towards her.

CHAPTER 6

*B*en couldn't stop glancing in Sarah's direction as he helped the ladies set up for a party. He never imagined that he'd see Sarah helping out with some of the basic jobs.

Several of the staff had told him that she always helped out with events, but actually seeing her perform mundane tasks in her crisp new outfit made him even more sure of his assessment of her.

Sweat dripped down his back as he finished placing the last of the chairs along the outer edge of the gazebo. He was surprised that such a small space could look so stylish with just a few decorations.

He watched Sarah make a quick excuse to her friends and rush back towards the main building. He was thinking of following her, but Lilith's hand on his arm stopped him.

"Thank you for helping out. You didn't have to."

He smiled down at her. "You're welcome. I figured it was the least I could do after…" He shook his head, unsure if he wanted to tell the woman that he was to blame for Sarah's previous predicament.

Lilith tilted her head and looked at him while he was silent. "What exactly are you here for?" she asked, crossing her arms over her chest as Heather stopped working and glanced up at him. Both of the women waited as he thought about his answer.

"I'm here strictly for assessment." It wasn't a lie, but not the whole truth either.

"Of?" Lilith asked, waiting.

"Didn't your boss tell you?" He decided to turn the tables.

"She's not one hundred percent sure herself."

"What was she told?" He leaned back against the railing and crossed his arms over his chest, matching her stance.

"Nothing. Well, until she called to confirm your reservations and she was told that someone from the main office was coming down and that we should accommodate him." Lilith smirked.

He nodded. "I was told to keep my trip under wraps as much as possible."

"Why?" Lilith asked as Heather walked over and tugged on the woman's sleeve, no doubt trying to get her to be quiet.

"No, we have a right to know. I mean, corporate has never sent a spy before. And he doesn't come across to me as spy material. I mean, he does have the whole sexy Bond thing going, but something in his eyes..." She moved closer. "So, spill."

His smile was quick. "I like you, Lilith. You're a

person who says what you want." He stood up and started to walk away.

"That's it?" she asked behind him.

"Yup." He glanced over his shoulder and winked at her. "We spies have to keep our secrets until the time is right." He jogged down the stairs and headed towards the dining room to grab a cool drink.

"Don't mess with Sarah. She has friends in low places if you know what I mean." Lilith smiled.

He chuckled and waved as he walked away. By the time he reached the dining room, he was parched. Sliding onto a stool at the bar, he ordered an ice tea and glanced around the room, wondering where Sarah was.

A small group of older people were sitting along the back wall, happily chatting as a young boy rushed around the room with an action figure in his hands. The kid was pretending to make the figure fly around the room as he made swishing noises.

Ben couldn't remember a time when he'd ever been allowed to be a kid like that, and it saddened him slightly. His parents had always expected him to be on his best behavior, which meant no running around and acting his age.

He glanced at the kid's mother and felt even more sadness creep in when he noticed her eyes warm as she looked at her son. He'd only ever seen pride in his parents' eyes once—the day he'd accepted the job at ERI. They weren't terrible people, just… devoid of compassion.

When he turned around to take another drink of his tea, he was surprised to see Sarah standing behind the bar.

"Thanks for your help out there." She leaned against

the bar and tilted her head slightly. "Is something wrong?" A slight frown played on her lips.

He shook his head, trying to clear the memories and lost feelings of family.

"No, just…" He took a deep breath. "Thinking."

She waited a moment before speaking. "I've been doing some of that myself. I think it would be best if I stayed on the island instead of going home tomorrow."

"Why?" He moved closer to her, wanting to reach out and take her hand in his.

She moved away, and he felt an emptiness spread, but then he realized she was walking around the bar. When she sat next to him, he couldn't stop from reaching out and touching her elbow slightly as she sat.

"I'm not sure I want to leave you alone all week with my staff."

He smiled. Even though she hadn't admitted it on the beach, she had just confirmed she had been listening in on his call.

"What about taking me with you?"

He felt her stiffen and her eyes squinted slightly.

"What?" It came out as a whisper.

"Well, since I've only booked my room through tonight, I'm sure there's a place I could stay on the mainland, so I can get a better feel for the area. I can always come back if needed."

She bit her bottom lip as she thought about it. He was lucky they were in a crowded room because just seeing the move made him want to do other fun things to her lip.

"Fine," she finally said, releasing a breath. "I usually catch the early ferry. It leaves at six." She started to get up, but he took her arm, holding her in place.

"I'm sorry about earlier." His eyes moved lower to her chest, remembering the sexy curves he'd witnessed earlier.

He heard her chuckle. "Don't be. All you did was catch me off guard." He dropped his hand as she stood up. As she started walking away, she glanced back at him. "It won't happen again."

With that, she turned and quickly left the room. A smile was plastered on his face for the rest of the evening.

He enjoyed another walk around the island but avoided the loud party going on at the gazebo. There was no way he wanted to get trapped again by a young woman trying to cure a bout of boredom. Several of his buddies back home would have gladly jumped at the chance, but Ben wasn't one of them.

Actually, he'd only been in a handful of relationships before. Two in high school and a few more serious ones in college. None of the women he'd dated had ever been good enough in his parents' eyes. He wondered what they would think of Sarah.

He made his way to the back kitchen area, curious to see if he could sneak some of the chocolate cake he'd heard Lilith talking about for the party.

He stepped into the kitchen door and saw Lilith and Adam wrapped around one another. He tried to turn back around before they saw him, but he wasn't quick enough.

They jumped apart quickly as Lilith's face turned beet red.

"Sorry," he mumbled, wishing he could disappear.

"No, don't be. It was either kiss her or put her over my knee," Adam said in his thick French accent, which only caused the redness in Lilith's cheeks to burn brighter, this time with anger.

"How dare—" she started to say, only to stop when Adam's eyebrows rose as he waited for her response. Instead, she made a sound deep from her chest, turned on her heels, and stormed out of the room.

"Now"—Adam turned to him— "what brings you to my kitchen?"

When Sarah opened the door to her rooms that night, she wasn't shocked to see Lilith sitting on her bed.

"What did he do this time?" she asked absentmindedly.

"He"—Lilith closed her eyes and let out a loud sigh— "kissed me."

"He… what?" Sarah burst out laughing and sat down on the bed next to her friend.

"All I did was tell him that Shania, the birthday girl, complained that his cake was a little dry."

"You did not!" Sarah sat up a little.

"Well, why wouldn't I? I mean, her parents spend a lot of money each year hosting her party with us. And… she did mention it to me."

Sarah shook her head slowly. "Of course, she did. Shania is a spoiled..." She held her breath and leaned back. "Never mind. You know better than to let a guest get between you and our staff."

"Trust me; it's not a guest that has gotten between that man and me."

"Yes, everyone who's seen you two within five feet of each other knows that." Sarah closed her eyes for a moment as she kicked off her shoes.

"So…" Lilith rolled over and propped her head on her arm. "What's between you and the sexy Mr. Rothschild?"

Sarah glanced over. "Nothing if I have any say about it." Then she turned towards her friend and mimicked her position. "I mean; the man is here to take my job!"

"Maybe," Lilith added softly as her eyes darted around the room, looking everywhere except at Sarah.

"What do you know?" She could tell her friend was hiding something.

"It's just that… Well, Heather and I were talking… after you left. And, well, we think he's actually here to check up on you."

"What?" She sat up quickly.

"You see, it's just that… Every question he asked us could in some way be turned back to you."

Sarah stood up and walked slowly to her window. It was too dark outside to see the view, and she knew that it wasn't much of one from her window since it overlooked the parking lot area.

"This changes things," she said to herself, not realizing she'd spoken out loud until Lilith spoke.

"How?"

Sarah turned around and crossed her arms over her chest. "No wonder he wanted to go to the mainland with me tomorrow."

Lilith rushed over to her, taking her shoulders in her hands. "He's going home with you?" Sarah could see the excitement in her friend's eyes and quickly shook her head from side to side.

"Correction. He was going to try and go home with me. But now that I know he's here for me…" She walked over to her closet and pulled out the overnight bag she always carried her toiletries home in. "I'm leaving tonight." She started tossing her stuff into the bag, not caring if she missed anything. Then she picked up her cell phone and shot a text to Jerry asking him to pick her up in half an hour.

"Wait." Lilith rushed over to her. "Why? How does this change things?"

She stopped for a moment to turn to her friend. "Now I realize he's been playing me." She could feel the anger building up and decided that the sooner she got off the island and away from Benjamin Rothschild, the better.

Swinging her bag over her shoulder, she slipped on her shoes and marched out of her room. "Tell the creep…" She stopped quickly, causing Lilith to bump into her shoulder and almost fall over.

"What?" Her friend looked at her blankly.

"I don't know… Make something up." She groaned as she turned back around.

"You can't do this to me," Lilith said, trying to keep up with her. "You know I'm no good at lies. I told Mark, the last guy you tried to avoid, that you had the mumps."

Sarah tried not to laugh. "Fine, say something, don't say something. Either way…" She reached the bottom of the stairs and pushed through the back doorway. When the cool night air hit her, she turned to Lilith, who had wrapped her arms around herself to keep warm.

"I'll see you on Friday." She leaned over and hugged her friend. She stopped before walking away. "The best way to deal with Adam is through his ego. The French are known for holding themselves in high esteem. All you need to do is… stroke his pride." She winked and smiled. "Oh, and if he tries to kiss you again…"

"Yes?" Lilith leaned closer.

"Hit him over the head with one of those cast iron frying pans." Sarah chuckled and turned around to walk down to her car.

She was sure Lilith used up her array of curse words, which consisted of only a handful, as she stormed back into the building. She knew her friend wasn't mad at her but at the sexy Frenchmen whom everyone knew had caught Lilith's attention the day he'd arrived.

Sarah knew firsthand that the feelings were mutual, since every time Lilith entered the room, Adam's accent grew thicker and the man stood taller.

Opening the trunk of her car, she tossed in her bag and walked around to the door. She was just about to open the door when a hand reached over and held her door shut.

"Going somewhere?"

She closed her eyes and groaned inwardly. Of course, she wouldn't be able to escape that easily.

Turning slowly around she nodded. "Yes, home."

"I thought we were leaving together tomorrow?" Ben said, keeping his hand on her door, blocking her in between the car and a solid wall of man.

"Something came up," she said briskly.

"Does that something have to do with me?" He moved slightly until he was leaning against her car.

Her eyes met his as she nodded.

"I can be packed in five minutes." He smiled down at her.

"Jerry's going to be here in two." Her chin went up slightly.

Ben nodded quickly. "Then two it is."

She wasn't given the opportunity to respond since he jogged quickly towards the main building.

She kept her eyes on his dark form as he disappeared towards the resort. He ran like he did it often. Maybe that's how he stayed so lean and in shape. A memory of his wet, naked body pressed up against her surfaced and she felt heat spread throughout her body, betraying her intentions.

Well, there was no way he would be back by the time Jerry arrived with the ferry.

She climbed into her car and started the engine, carefully backing up and positioning her car at the end of the dock. Sitting in the dark, she tried to keep her mind off the memory of how nice it had been to be kissed and held.

Too long. She'd gone almost six months without going out on a date. Why had she let herself go this long?

Deciding it was past time to go out, she was determined to call up one of her old friends and hit the town soon.

Her focus was drawn ahead when she noticed the spotlights on the ferry heading her way. Smiling slightly, she looked behind her and noticed that Ben's car was still parked in the same spot.

Oh, well, she thought as she put her car into gear and watched Jerry maneuver the flatboat into position. Just as Jerry was lowering the gate, her back passenger door swung open and Ben tossed his bags into her back seat. Then he opened the front door and climbed in beside her.

"I hope it's okay, but I figured I'd leave my rental here and ride with you." He smiled over at her. "Since you decided to leave early."

Her eyes narrowed as she glared at him. Then Jerry

knocked on her window, causing her to jump. Rolling down the glass, she smiled up at the man.

"Hey, you okay?" Jerry asked, glancing at Ben.

"Sure." She reached out and touched his hand as it rested on her window. "Everything's fine."

"Okay. I figured something was up since you wanted to leave early." His eyes moved once more to Ben.

"Sarah was just so excited to show me the nightlife in Silver Cove," Ben added.

She glanced up at Jerry and nodded. "I figured I could show him around and take him to Ed's for some pizza."

Jerry smiled. "A slice of Ed's pizza and a cold beer does sound good." Jerry stood aside and waved her onto the ferry.

"You're pretty good at that," Ben said after she pulled her parking brake on.

"What?" She glanced at him.

"Lying." The side of his lips curved up.

"I could say the same about you." Her chin went up as she got out of her car.

CHAPTER 7

*B*en stood against the railing and watched the wind blow Sarah's hair. The chill in the night air caused her cheeks to flush, giving them a slight pink hue.

She was leaning on the railing, looking out into the dark water. She kept her eyes away from him and he wondered what he'd done to cause the conflict he could see in her eyes now.

When he leaned closer to her, she leaned away.

"Are you going to tell me what's wrong?" he asked, brushing a finger down the outside of her jacket. He felt her stiffen.

After a moment of silence, she turned to him. "Why are you here?"

He frowned slightly. "Because it's my job."

"And what exactly is your job?"

"I'm general manager of…"

"Yes, I know your current title," she broke in. "What I'm asking is what job are you doing in Silver Cove?"

"The one I was asked to do." He smiled and shook his head slightly, stopping the next question from leaving her lips. "Sarah, I wish I could tell you more, but I can't. You'll just have to trust me."

"Why would I?" She turned around and leaned against the railing, crossing her arms over her chest. "I just met you a few days ago."

He nodded. "Fair enough. So, why don't we use the next few days to get to know one another better?"

When she squinted her eyes at him, he continued. "What do you say to an agreement?"

She tilted her head, looking interested. "Of?"

"While we are of the island, we leave our jobs behind."

Her eyebrows shot up. "That sounds fair, but don't you still have work to do?"

He smiled. "I think I can take a few days to enjoy myself. Besides, I've already made up my mind and was told to take a week to further think about it." He rolled his eyes.

"You've already made up…"

"Ut, ut…" He moved closer and placed his fingers lightly over her lips. "We're technically off the island." He smiled and could feel her lips curve up under his finger. "So, can we agree to just enjoy ourselves for the next few days?"

His eyes met hers and he watched the process of her making up her mind. When his finger dropped from her lip, she smiled even more.

"I suppose it would be nice to find out a little more about you," she hummed.

He chuckled and moved closer to her. "Now, I suggest

we start…" He leaned closer to her lips, but at that moment, the boat made a sharp turn.

"We're at the docks," she whispered as she dropped her arms from his. He'd been so focused on watching her lips, that he hadn't realized she'd reached up and held onto him.

"Later," he promised.

As they made their way back to the car, Jerry jogged past them and unlatched the gate.

"It's good to know it wasn't my driving that caused you to lose your lunch last time," he joked. "I'll see you on Thursday." He waved as Sarah backed off of the deck.

"Bye." She waved and put the car into drive.

"So." He glanced at her and tilted his body a little. "Is there anything between you two?"

"Who?" She quickly glanced at him as she pulled out of the dirt road. "Jerry?" She chuckled. "I suppose at one time we thought about it, but then he started dating one of my cousins and… well… we became friends and nothing more."

He felt instantly relieved.

"How did you put it back on the beach? Why would I want or need anyone else after I've played with you?" She smiled over at him as she turned onto the paved road.

They sat in silence during the short drive into town. For the most part, it was too dark to see anything. Once they hit the outskirts of the town of Silver Cove, everything changed.

He'd never seen a town as picturesque before. There were enough lights shining on the side of the street that he could see the charm of the older two-story buildings that lined the main thoroughfare.

Sarah drove slowly enough that he could read the signs that hung over the doors. So many small businesses and bed-and-breakfasts.

"Do these interfere with East Haven?" he asked, absentmindedly.

When she just chuckled in response, he turned and looked at her.

"Seriously?" She waited and when he just continued to look at her, she sighed and shook her head from side to side.

"East Haven is in a whole different bracket."

He thought about it and realized she was right. He'd never really thought about the caliber of clientele that booked rooms at the resort.

"You could stay at any of these B&B's for under a hundred a night." She nodded to a very large house at the corner of the street. Its old-world charm was accented impressively with stone and a tall white chimney. Wide decks reached around the entire building, making him think of long lazy evenings drinking iced tea and watching the sunset.

"That's the biggest one." She stopped in front of the impressive building and he noticed a sign out front with gold letters—Carmen's B&B. "Carmen runs a clean place. If any of these could steal customers, this would be the place." She started driving again.

"You must know everyone in town," he said as he took in everything about the small town.

"For the most part. We have a lot of seasonal residents that I'm not too familiar with."

Just then everything about the small sleepy town

changed. They had crossed double train tracks and were thrust into a small old-time metropolis.

"Wow," he exclaimed.

"Yeah. It throws you off the first time you see it, doesn't it?"

He could only nod his head.

"Most people don't realize that Silver Cove has been around for almost two centuries. The old-town charm has, of course, been updated in the past few years." She stopped in front of a well-lit building with a sign that said Ed's Pizzeria hanging above the door. "Well, I'm a woman of her word." She reached over to open her door, but he stopped her.

"That was never under question." He smiled and pulled her closer. "There's just one thing I need to get out of the way." He tugged a little more until she was almost in his lap. When his lips met hers, he felt the same zing he'd felt on the beach that first time he'd kissed her.

He'd never experienced the shock of an electric fence, but he was pretty sure he was getting the same spark of power from her lips. His hands roamed slowly over her as her mouth explored his.

He could feel his body's instant reaction to her soft body pushed up against his. When a group of loud teens walked by the car, he felt her jolt and move away.

Instantly, he felt the loss of her warmth and softness.

"There, now I might be able to concentrate on sitting across from you without dreaming about doing that." He smiled at her as she brushed her fingers through her hair.

"This wasn't supposed to happen, you know." She glanced at him sideways.

"What?" He couldn't stop smiling at her, so he turned

his head and glanced out at a group of people walking into the pizzeria.

"This." He heard her release a slow breath. "I wasn't going to let you play me."

He turned back to her. "Play?"

She closed her eyes for a brief moment. "Let's get some food. I'm starving, and I don't want to have this conversation on an empty stomach."

Before he could reply, she was out of the car, closing down any rebuttal. Yes, they were definitely going to finish this conversation.

Sarah closed her eyes and moaned deep in her chest as the hot cheese melted in her mouth, sending every single one of her taste buds on a happy dance.

"Best pizza ever!" she said once she'd completely chewed the bite.

"It is pretty good." She could tell he was holding back. He'd had a strange look on his face since she'd mentioned the game he was playing with her.

She knew, just knew there was something else behind those dark eyes that he wasn't telling her. He'd owned up to keeping his secrets about why he was there, but there was something else he wasn't telling her. Something bigger. About himself.

"You aren't married, are you?" she blurted out after finishing off her first slice.

He'd just taken a drink of his beer and began to choke on the swallow. She quickly got up and started slapping him on his back.

"G-god!" he stuttered out once his airway was clear. "Of course not!" He frowned over at her. "Is that what you think of me? That I'd keep something that big from you?"

She walked over and slid back into her side of the booth as she shrugged her shoulders. "I don't know you that well."

He took another big sip of his beer.

"I've never been married. Or engaged, for that matter." He eyed her. "You?"

She shook her head as she pulled another slice onto her plate. "I was engaged to Kevin, the first love of my life, but since he was a chicken and I was six, I doubt that counts."

She enjoyed the sound of his laughter. "I bet you would have made a cute bride for Kevin."

She smiled back at him. "What did you do after Harvard?" She leaned back in the booth and tucked her legs underneath her as she bit into the warm pizza.

"This and that. Until I got picked up by Elite." He finished off his second slice and reached for another.

"Any traveling?" She knew how to get answers from people. She was usually really good at it, but he just wasn't cooperating.

"Some, here and there." He took a bite.

"Any outside of the country," she asked and was unnerved when he just nodded in reply. "Brothers or sisters?"

This is where he set his pizza down and looked at her. "A much younger sister. You?"

Then she saw it. What he'd been hiding from her. The silent pain she'd seen behind those dark eyes. Setting her half-eaten slice down, she leaned closer.

"No, I'm an only child. Tell me about your sister."

His eyes narrowed as he reached for his beer. He downed a quarter of it in one large swallow, and his dark eyes met hers.

"Bella is sixteen."

Sarah's eyebrows rose. "Much younger." He nodded in agreement but didn't continue. "And?"

He reached for his beer again but changed his mind and pushed the almost empty glass away instead.

"And… my parents had me when they were young, shortly after they had graduated college."

"That's not too young," she broke in.

"According to them, it was." His eyes grew darker. "Funny, my father was my age when I was born." He leaned back in his chair and his jaw tightened slightly. "One of my first memories was of my parents dropping me off at my grandparents' house for the summer, so they could spend a few months in Italy to escape the mundane life of parenting. When they returned, it took less than a year before I was shipped off to a boarding school in England."

She nodded, realizing that she had an explanation for the slight accent she heard that first night when he'd been sick.

"How long were you there?"

He reached for his beer and downed the rest of the dark liquid. "Four years. Then my grandparents stepped in and demanded that I learn the Rothschild way."

"Which is?"

"Honor, integrity, loyalty." He sneered. She could see he was almost laughing at some private joke.

"I suppose those are good qualities."

The short burst of laughter that escaped him told her more than his words did.

"Don't you agree with them?"

"It's not a matter of whether I agree. It's a matter of how the rest of my family actually lives. You know the old saying: do as I say, not as I do."

She nodded, reaching over and picking up her glass of wine. She'd only taken a few sips during dinner, but now, with his story going, she realized she wanted the relaxation that always came with a glass.

"Well, my parents are king and queen of ignoring their own advice. My father always talked about honor, but I found out early in junior high about some of the shady deals he'd taken part in. My mother spoke often of integrity, but with the same breath, she talked down about the ladies at the country club. Loyalty." He reached for his glass, only to frown at the emptiness and push it aside. "They are only loyal to their children if they can see a profit or benefit to themselves. Bella," he sighed deeply, "is a different story."

"How so?" She took another sip of the dark red liquid and enjoyed the warmth that spread through her. He picked up a glass of water and took a drink.

"Well, for all of their misgivings about raising me, they've done a complete turnaround for her. It's as if they decided to actually be parents for the first time in their lives."

"Are you close with her?"

His eyes focused on her once more. "I try to be."

"But?"

He shrugged and picked up another slice. "I'm in Boston and they've recently moved to northern Vermont, so I don't see her as often as I'd like. We stay connected, but... it's not the same." She watched him smile for the first time since he'd started talking about his family. "We have a standard Saturday morning Skype session that our parents don't know about."

"Why would you have to hide talking to your sister from your parents?"

The smile quickly fell away from his lips. "They don't approve of me talking to her; they think I might be giving her advice."

She couldn't help the burst of sarcastic laughter that escaped her. "Sorry."

"No, what?" The corners of his lips turned upwards.

Her hair fell around her shoulders as she shook her head from side to side. She finished off her wine as he waited for her to say what she wanted to say.

"It's just... I mean, isn't that what big brothers are for? Giving advice and protecting their sisters?" She leaned back and relaxed. "I always dreamed about having a big brother or sister. Someone who could show me the ropes in life."

"What about your mother?"

She rolled her eyes at him as a snort escaped her. "It's obvious that you haven't met the woman yet."

CHAPTER 8

He could tell that Sarah was nervous as she drove the few blocks to her mother's shop. She kept tapping the steering wheel and taking slow deep breaths.

From the outside, Serenity's Attic looked like every other building along the street. What set it aside was that, instead of having a crisp white exterior like its neighbors, the entire lower floor was painted with sun and moon designs in bright blue and yellow. White bulb lights hung on the eaves, making the store almost glow in the dark night. The front doors were painted a bright purple with stars painted into the deep color.

Sarah parked her car in front of the building and turned to him. "I'd like to say I'm sorry in advance for anything you see or hear in the next few days."

"I think I can handle hanging around a free-spirited woman, especially knowing she's the woman that raised you."

He could see her eyes soften before she turned away. "Crystal is… a little more than free-spirited."

He reached over and took her hand in his. "Sarah, I've explained my parents to you. Trust me, after being ignored by them, I believe any parent who gives a damn is an improvement."

He watched her shoulders rise and fall. Then she squared up as her chin rose. "Okay." She turned back to him. "But, you've been warned."

His smile was quick, following hers. Still holding her hand, he leaned in and placed a soft kiss on her lips to show her he understood.

When they walked through the front doors, a bell chimed. The strong smell of incense hit him. He'd had a college roommate once whose girlfriend had burned the sweet-smelling sticks every time she entered their dorm room. She'd claimed it had been to get rid of the smell of body odor and feet that every dorm room smelled of.

The aroma instantly brought back good memories from those days, causing him to smile. He glanced around the store and took everything in.

The front of the store was reserved for local organic produce. Two large glass refrigerators stood right inside the doors. One was full of milk, butter, and cheese, while the other was filled with various organic meats.

Jars of incense were next, along with rows of candles. Liquid-filled jars with brightly colored labels sat behind them and he assumed they were filled with scented oils. On the other side of the store were star charts, T-shirts, scarves, armbands, jewelry, and other items lined up on the longer wall.

Bags, scarfs, and beads hung from the ceiling, which was painted a deep blue and was covered with more stars.

He'd been in shops like this before, but instead of the normal clutter, everything seemed organized and in its own place. He glanced over at Sarah and knew that it was her doing.

Just then, a blonde woman walked in from the back room. Instantly, he knew it was Crystal, Sarah's mother. The woman's long blonde hair lay down over her shoulders, reaching all the way to her hips. There was a bright green and blue wreath sitting on the crown of her head. She was wearing a long flowing skirt, much like the one he'd seen Sarah in that first night. This one was dark blue with big bright yellow flowers on it. Her white top fell off her bare left shoulder and several necklaces of beads covered her chest.

He could tell the woman was comfortable in her own skin.

"Serenity!" The woman dropped a small box she'd been carrying and rushed forward to hug her daughter. "I wasn't expecting you until the morning."

"Yeah, well…" He watched Sarah blush a little. "Crystal, this is Benjamin Rothschild. He works for Elite."

The woman turned towards him, keeping her arm around Sarah's shoulders. Her eyes roamed over him. At first, she had a frown on her lips as her eyes took in everything. When she zeroed in on his eyes, however, a smile slowly formed on her lips.

"Welcome." She dropped her arm from around her daughter and rushed forward to engulf him in a hug.

Sarah closed her eyes, rolled her head back in embarrassment, and whispered, "Oh my god."

He couldn't explain it but having this stranger wrap her arms around him felt like the first motherly act he'd experienced in his entire twenty-seven years. He held onto Sarah's mother for a moment before his mind cleared.

"Serenity?" His eyes moved to Sarah's as she once more closed them on an embarrassed groan.

Crystal took a step from him but kept her hands on his arms. "It's a real pleasure to meet you." Her smile held a hint of mischief. "How long will you be staying with us?"

"Just this week." He glanced back at Sarah and mouthed, "Serenity?"

To which she quickly mouthed back, "Shut up," causing him to smile.

"Crystal," Sarah said, causing her mother to turn towards her and place her hands on her hips like every mother had done at one point.

"Will you stop calling me that," she demanded in a friendly voice before taking Ben's arm in her hands and walking him towards the back of the shop. "Serenity started calling me that in third grade." She tilted her head towards him and whispered. "I think it makes her feel more grown up."

He tried to stifle the chuckle that escaped him. "I called my father Mr. Rothschild for an entire year after returning home from school."

Crystal's laughter was soft and warm. She continued to talk to him as she guided him to a large back room. Here, there were more beads, scarves, and candles, but these were all personally used and to Crystal's tastes.

Sarah followed them, quietly gripping as she went.

"Mother," she finally said after he'd been persuaded to sit and have a cup of chive tea.

"Yes, dear?" Crystal said, too busy fixing them tea to give Sarah her full attention.

"Ben is going to need the room upstairs this week."

"Oh?" Crystal finally stopped and turned back towards them. "I assumed that you'd be staying with Serenity." She tilted her head, looked him in the eyes, and said, "I see." She nodded her head and smiled. "Too soon, I suppose." She dipped her chin and turned back around to Sarah. "I'm sorry. I've been working on the upstairs apartment and I'm afraid it's in a rather dismal state." She poured the tea into three mugs and walked over to sit next to him. "But you're always welcome to stay with us instead. There's plenty of room."

"I couldn't..." he started to say, only to have her break in.

"Nonsense. We occasionally let out our rooms to friends, don't we, Serenity?"

He glanced towards Sarah, who was still standing, leaning against the door frame as she sipped her tea. After nodding her head, she added, "There are four guest rooms."

"Thanks," he said. He wasn't sure how the week was going to pan out, as he would be sleeping under the same roof as the woman he wanted and her mother.

Sarah walked in front of Ben as she climbed the outside stairs to the old house that had been in her family for generations. To her, it was just home. To everyone in the small town of Silver Cove, it was a historic site that demanded to be preserved.

"Welcome to Holley Hall." She motioned for him to follow her.

"Wow," Ben said from behind her. "You live here?"

She turned, her hand resting on the stair railing. "Almost all my life." She turned back and started climbing again. The staircase was stone with strong black iron railings that twisted into ornamental pots at the bottom. Each one held small decorative bushes. The covered front porch was long and wide and held some of her fondest memories outside of East Haven. "My great-great-grandfather built it in the 1700s." She stopped at the wide front glass door. "It was deemed a historic site a few years back before my grandparents passed."

The three-story colonial home was still painted the creamy yellow it had been when it had first been built. The black shutters had been replaced with new ones when she was young, as had the white windows.

Ben stopped next to her, shuffled his bag on his shoulder, and glanced around. "Impressive. Serenity." His slight smile caused her to glare at him.

"Only my family calls me that." She growled it out as a warning, to which he chuckled lightly and nodded.

"Point taken." His eyes moved back to their surroundings.

She followed his gaze. There were old rockers, a porch swing, and more potted plants here. Ben wondered what it must have been like centuries ago when carts were pulled by horses and gas lamps lit the streets in front.

"You think this is nice…" She reached down and opened the door, swinging it wide as she motioned for him to enter.

As he stepped over the threshold, he let out a low whistle. She moved next to him and smiled. She loved watching people's eyes as they took in the beautiful staircase her great-great-grandfather had built for the woman he'd loved.

There was a wide entryway and high arches with decorative molding. The walls here were the same yellow as outside, accenting the crisp whiteness of all the glorious molding.

The stairs themselves were a dark cherry, and they shined as if new, as did the floors on the entire main level. The staircase twisted at an angle, leading your eyes towards the massive windows on the second floor. There was a wide window seat that ran the entire length of the wall, which was as comfortable as it looked.

On either side of the stairs were white doors with frosted windows. The one to the left led to the kitchen and dining rooms, the door to the right to a sunroom and study. There was a formal sitting room directly to the left and a small library and study to the right.

"It looks like it came off the cover of *Better Homes and Gardens*," Ben said beside her.

"Yeah." She chuckled. She'd heard the same statement so many times in her lifetime.

"It's not what I'd expect from the two ladies who live here."

She turned and frowned at him. "What does that mean?"

"Only that I don't really see any of your or your mother's personalities here."

She slowly nodded. "We reserve our tastes for our own rooms."

"I'm sure you do." He smiled down at her.

"Come on, the guest's rooms are on the second floors." She walked towards the stairs.

"How about after, you give me a tour?" he asked, following her up the stairs.

"Sure."

"Tell me about this house. You said your great-great-grandfather built it?"

"Yup. George Holley was the town doctor. The first in Silver Cove. He moved here fresh out of medical school and married the mayor's daughter, Mildred, whom he had fallen in love with the first day in town." When they reached the top of the stairs, she turned and looked down with a smile. "George built the staircase first and then built the rest of house around it, claiming the staircase is like the spine of the house." She chuckled. "I would have loved to meet the man." Letting out a sigh, she continued down the wide hallway towards the right. "There are four rooms on this floor, two on this side, two on the other. You can have your pick of them. There is a bathroom at the end of each hallway." She pointed to the door at the end of each side. "The linen closets are the smaller doors; anything you might need is there. Extra blankets, towels, whatever." She opened the small wooden door and showed him the well-stocked closet. "The first room is my favorite." She opened the door to the left and watched as Ben walked in and looked around.

The blue room, as she liked to call it, was the biggest of the four rooms. Its wide windows overlooked the back garden area and it was the farthest from the street noises. The classic wallpaper with small blue hydrangea flower designs was a good mix between masculine and feminine, making the room attractive for either sex.

There was a large four-poster bed, one of the originals in the house, which sat directly across from the wide window and its window seat. As with each room, a small desk and a flat-screen TV sat on opposite walls.

Ben walked over and set his bag down on the bed. "I'll take this one."

"Don't you want to see the others?"

He turned to her. "When I see something I like; I tend to make up my mind quickly."

Heat flooded her face, so she turned around quickly and walked to the end of the hallway. "Here's the bathroom." She opened the door to the larger room. "Its twin is at the end of the hallway." Ben stepped in and looked around.

There was an oversized white steel tub that sat in front of three long stained-glass windows. The shower had been redone just a few years ago. The stone walls had been replaced with a lighter tile and glass doors had been added along with updated shower heads. To the left sat a double-sink vanity. The toilet had its own private closet area.

"The bathrooms must have been added later."

"Yes, I'm told my grandfather remodeled and added the updated plumbing and electric." She moved to the next guest room. Its creamy yellow walls matched the exterior and entry walls. The bed was smaller, but still as classic. As they moved to the next two rooms, she continued to talk about the home and her family history.

"I assume you and your mother's rooms are on the third floor?"

"Yes, that's where our personalities are allowed to shine." She turned to him and stopped at the top of the stairs. The narrow staircase leading to the third floor was closed off by a solid wood door to the left. "We have our own entrances outside." She started walking down the stairs, running her fingers on the smooth railing. "Since I'm only here a few days a week, I don't mind living down the hall from my mother." She stopped at the bottom of the stairs.

"What do you do with all this space?" He glanced around.

She tilted her head, unsure of his question. "We use it."

His smirk told her that he didn't believe her. "I'll show you." She opened the left doorway and walked into the well-used dining room, heading towards the stocked kitchen.

"I thought upstairs was impressive." He leaned against the high bar area while she moved over to the small wine fridge under the bar and pulled out one of her favorite local labels. Then she walked over and took down two glasses.

"My grandfather remodeled it when I was in grade school." She handed him the glass and turned to pour her own. "He even let me pick out the tile." She smiled at the bright teal backsplash. She'd believed that the bright color would be her mark on the otherwise white kitchen. The hints of cherry wood gave the large room a warm feeling, but that hint of brightness made the room more cheerful.

"Nice. I love the splash of color. Which just proves you had a talent early on."

She'd picked out barstools with the same colors, as well as placed several decorative bowls and vases around the room.

She leaned against the counter and took a sip of her wine, looking at Ben and trying to get a better idea about him. So far, all she knew was that he'd practically raised himself, something she could relate to. Actually, it was the main thing that was drawing her to him because it made them likeminded. She knew he had a sister and where he'd gone to school and, obviously, who he worked for, but beyond that, the man sitting before her was a complete mystery.

"What?" He sat down in one of the stools and looked at her as he drank his wine. "You look as if you're trying to solve a puzzle."

She set her glass down and crossed her arms over her chest. "I am."

He set his glass down and quickly moved to his feet in front of her. His hands rested on her shoulders as he took another step to her. "I'm no puzzle to solve. I come from a pretty screwed-up family. I was raised with money, not love. I'm a hard worker and have proven I can make my own way in life, and when I see something I want…" He leaned forward, giving her time to step aside or tell him no. But her eyes locked with his darker ones, giving him permission. "I go after it."

CHAPTER 9

When his lips brushed against hers, he felt his knees almost buckle out from under him. He'd kissed her a few times now, and each time, the feelings inside him grew to almost a swell.

Her arms wrapped around his shoulders as she moved closer to him. Now, her body was pressed tightly against his, causing his body to react to her softness. His fingers tightened on her shoulders before moving up to tangle in the mass of blonde hair that fell around her face.

The richness of the wine was on the tip of her tongue, making him want to dip deeper for another taste. When her legs wrapped around him, he hoisted her up until she sat on the edge of the countertop. His hands were snaking down to pull those sexy slacks down her hips when they both heard the front door open.

"Serenity?" a very deep male voice called out.

She jumped down and pushed him aside quickly. Whoever he was, she didn't want him to know what they'd been doing in the kitchen.

She straightened her hair and shirt and then picked up her wine just as a very tall, blond man walked into the kitchen like he'd been there many times before.

"There you are. I saw your car out front when I got home and thought I'd—" The man stopped when Ben walked over to pick up his wine glass, blocking the man's view from Sarah.

"I'm Rowan." The man held out his hand. "Serenity's cousin."

Relief flooded Ben. He took a gulp of his wine and then set his glass down to shake the man's hand. It was a firm handshake that told Ben a lot about the man.

"Ben Rothschild." He offered nothing more.

"Ben works for Elite," Sarah added as she finished off her glass of wine.

"Oh?" Rowan walked over and wrapped his arm around Sarah's shoulders in a protective manner.

He could see the easiness between the pair and wished he had cousins or siblings he felt that comfortable with.

"Ben's in town until Monday and needed a place to stay." The fact that Sarah felt like she owed her cousin an explanation made him pause.

"I figured I'd come back to the mainland with Sarah, so we could get to know one another better." He picked up the wine bottle, poured her a little more, and then did the same for his glass, finishing off the bottle.

"How are you liking Silver Cove so far?" Rowan dropped his arm from around Sarah and then grabbed himself a beer from the small fridge.

"So far, so good. We had dinner at Ed's and then stopped by Serenity's Attic." He moved next to Sarah and leaned close to her. "The house is impressive. Do you live around here?"

Rowan smiled. "Across the way. When our great-great-grandfather built this place, he built two more on the street, one for each of his sons. And since our mothers are sisters and the last in the Holley line…"

"Why don't we move into the sitting room?" Sarah pushed off from the counter, putting space between her and him.

He followed them through the large impressive dining room with its long gleaming table and chairs, past the staircase, and through another glass door. He would have never described the room as a sitting room. It was massive. There was a sunken area that housed two identical cream leather sofas. A wide stone fireplace sat at the end of them with long, wide windows on either side. Even with the darkness outside, he could tell that the room would be light and inviting during the daytime.

Sarah and Rowan walked over and sat side by side on the sofa, leaving him to take the opposite one by himself.

He watched as Sarah kicked off her shoes and tucked her feet underneath her, leaning into her cousin comfortably.

"Rowan just moved back from Chicago, where he'd been running his own practice. He's a doctor like our George was." The smile that flooded her lips told him she was very proud of her cousin.

"I'm trying to reopen George's practice here. Someday, the Holley Clinic will open its doors again."

Rowan wrapped his arm around Sarah's shoulder once more and she settled next to him.

"Do your parents still live next door?" he asked, wishing for a beer instead of the almost empty wine glass.

"No, they moved to Florida two years ago. The place sat empty until Serenity here persuaded me to move back a few months ago."

The conversation moved further into their family history and the house's history. A little over an hour later, Sarah's mother walked in, carrying a plate of chips and fruit along with another bottle of wine. She sat next to Ben, turning the conversation back to Sarah and Rowan's childhood days.

He loved listening to the stories of how they had grown up together, raised as if they were brother and sister. From what he could gather, Crystal's sister was the complete opposite of her. She had been more conservative in raising her son, but family had obviously been important.

He caught himself daydreaming several times during their stories about being part of their world.

He noticed Sarah's head rolling back several times and when he glanced down at his watch, he was shocked to realize it was one in the morning.

"I think we'd better get some rest." He stood up, reaching for his empty wine glass.

"No, leave it," Crystal said. "I'll clean up." She waved him off. "Go on up. I'm sure Serenity has big plans to show you around town tomorrow. If you get a chance, swing by the store again and I'll introduce you around myself."

He nodded and held out his hand for Sarah to take so he could help her up. When she was standing beside him, half leaning on him, he held his hand out to Rowan. "It was nice meeting you."

"Likewise. If you get a moment, have Serenity show you where our great-great-grandfather's clinic was."

He nodded, then wrapped his arm around Sarah and started walking towards the stairs.

"I think he likes you," Sarah said close to his ear.

"That's good. He seems like a nice enough guy."

Her warm chuckle sounded like heaven in his ears, as did her soft body next to his.

"Everyone likes Rowan. Rowan is the all-American male. He was the star quarterback who dated the lead cheerleader, captain of every sport he ever played. He had perfect grades and anything he ever wanted."

He stopped her at the top of the stairs. "You make it sound like it was a bad thing."

She frowned a little and shook her head slightly, tightening her grip on his shirt to steady herself. "No! I love Rowan. He's like my brother."

"Then?"

She took a deep breath and slowly released it. "There's more pain behind those eyes than even I know. His girlfriend, the cheerleader, was killed."

"What happened?" He steered her towards his room.

"No one knows. It was the night of his sixteenth birthday party. They found her shortly before his party began. She'd been…" Sarah closed her eyes and leaned a little more on his shoulder. "Torn apart."

He shook his head and glanced back towards the stairs. He was having a hard time picturing the man he'd just spent the last few hours talking to going through something like that so early in life.

"Did you know her?"

"Not really. I mean, we were in the same classes

before… She was a year younger than Rowan. But we weren't in the same circles." She walked over and sat on the edge of the massive bed, leaning back on her elbows as she glanced up at the canopy.

He walked over, picked up her feet, and set them in his lap, absentmindedly rubbing her insteps as she talked.

"I wasn't… well, she was two-faced. Rowan never discovered the other side to her like I did. Obviously, someone else had."

"What happened to make you think that way about her?" She closed her eyes with pleasure when his thumb pushed into the ball of her foot. She rolled her head on her shoulders and leaned further back on the bed.

"My mother was in charge of buying my clothes all through grade school." Her eyes moved to his and he nodded when he got her meaning. "Yeah, you could see how that wouldn't make me the most popular kid. Then, she pulled me out to homeschool me and I was never given the chance to show everyone my own style throughout my junior and high school years. By the time I went back into public school, Lori had already been murdered."

"Was Rowan homeschooled?"

Sarah snorted out a laugh and rolled until she could look at him more directly. "Are you kidding? My Aunt Genie would have never allowed that. Nor would my Uncle Charles."

"Why not?" he asked, running his hand over her thigh. Her eyes closed, and he thought he heard a slight moan escape her lips.

"Let's just put it this way. My aunt and uncle moved into this century, along with everyone else in this small town. My mother, however, still doesn't believe women should wear bras or buy their bread from stores instead of baking it fresh every day from scratch.

His chuckle was low as his hand continued to roam over her. "I like homemade bread." He leaned closer to her until her eyes focused on his.

"I suppose you're fond of women who don't wear bras too," she said as her hand moved up to his shoulder, neither holding him nor pushing him away.

His eyes roamed over her slowly. "Either way is sexy as hell when it's the right woman."

How was Sarah supposed to concentrate on staying distant from Ben when she kept sinking into his dark eyes? His fingers brushed over her softly, causing her system to relax even more. Maybe it was the extra wine she'd enjoyed or the fact that she'd been up since four that morning, but she felt like she couldn't move a muscle from her spot on his bed.

Her mind was foggy and the only thought she could hold onto was that his hands felt good on her. She tried to focus on his eyes as he hovered over her, but then he moved closer and her lids shut as his lips brushed against her own. The kiss was one of the softest she'd ever experienced in her life. And she'd enjoyed plenty of kisses before. Even with Ben. This one was different. Instead of want or a bubble of desire, this kiss spoke of soft lazy days spent making love slowly.

She'd never experienced anything like that before and desperately wanted to. Her mind drifted off, dreaming of what it would be like to spend a warm lazy day in the huge bed, naked, skin to skin with him.

She woke when a streak of sunlight slanted across her eyes. Her hand moved up to block it, but she found that both of her hands were currently being crushed under a very warm body. Cracking one eye open, she looked directly into Ben's smiling face.

"So, all it takes to wake you is a ray of sunshine?" He shifted, making her realize that he'd pulled off his shirt sometime during the night. Now, his skin was pressed against her hands and chest. Glancing down, her eyebrows rose when she realized he'd left her clothes in place.

"I must have fallen asleep," she said, looking back up at him.

"Hmm," he agreed, moving his free hand up and brushing a clump of her hair away from her face. "Like the dead. You dropped off pretty fast."

"Well, it had been a very long day." He smiled. "Plus, all that wine."

"You don't have to make excuses. I'm just thankful I got to hold you throughout the night."

What was she supposed to say to that? Most men she'd been involved with hated snuggling. Before or after sex. And they hadn't even done anything besides kiss!

"Umm," she started, only to stop when he chuckled.

"You look like you're trying to figure out how to tell the teacher your dog ate your homework."

Her eyes narrowed. "You think this is funny?"

He nodded slightly and laughed again. "If you could see your face, you would too." He rolled over, taking Sarah with him until she rested on his chest, her hair pooling around them as she glared down into his dark eyes.

His arms were now wrapped around her waist tightly, holding her in place.

"I didn't mean to scare you. I only meant that it was nice having you around to keep me warm."

She gave him a smirk, showing him that she didn't believe him. "I didn't mean to fall asleep on you."

His hand roamed to her hips, holding her closer. She could feel his hardness pressed up against her hips, which caused something to heat deep inside her. Desire shot through her quickly when his fingers brushed her sides, under her arms.

"Ben." It came out as a whisper.

"Hmm." His eyes were locked on her lips. She knew she could easily fall into a pattern of wanting him, and somehow that scared her.

Pulling back slightly, she looked into his eyes, her hands resting on his bare chest. She could feel the muscles tighten as she kept him waiting.

Finally, she leaned closer and whispered, "You need a shower."

She hadn't expected the burst of laughter, or his arms wrapping around her once more as he rolled them off the bed. When they were finally standing, his arms were still holding her tight. "What are the chances of you joining me for a quick rinse?"

She tilted her head and gave him a look that clearly told him her thoughts on the subject.

His smile grew. "Can't blame a guy for trying." His head dipped down and he brushed his lips across hers quickly. "Shower, then breakfast. I'm starved."

She took a step back and wrapped her arms around herself. The loss of his heat next to her body made her realize just how cool the morning air was in the room. "Then we're heading out." She turned and walked towards the door. "I hope you packed a pair of hiking boots in that bag." She waited at the door for him to respond.

"I have my running shoes, which should do. Why?"

She wiggled her eyebrows. "It's a secret. Wear jeans and bring a jacket." She turned to go.

"Sarah." His voice stopped her before she could close the door. She glanced over her shoulder and waited. "Thanks. For letting me stay here and for staying last night." She could only nod since her throat had closed up on her.

As she rushed up the narrow staircase leading to her rooms, her mind kept rushing over their conversations. Since the moment she'd met him, he'd done nothing but show her kindness and interest. Why?

If he was really here to take her dream job, wouldn't he be… well, something else?

Here, on the third floor, her mother's personality was allowed to shine. The bright yellow halls always made Sarah feel welcomed in the space. Large paintings her mother had done years ago hung on every available spot.

Clear and smoky crystals hung in the windows, casting rainbows in every direction. All the window coverings had been removed years ago. Since they towered over all of their neighbors' homes, there was no one to see anything that went on in the upper floors. Besides, her mother wasn't that concerned about her privacy.

Two of the rooms on this level had been turned into sitting rooms so that off each hallway sat a bedroom and an attached sitting room. Sarah had taken the west wing since she tended to sleep in when she was home. Her mother took the other side since she loved the early morning light.

She was just about to enter her bedroom when her mother's door burst open. "I thought I heard you," her mother said walking out, covered only in a bright blue towel. Her long blonde hair was wrapped up by a green towel. She walked towards Sarah, but halfway to her, she stopped. "Oh…" Her mother's head tilted slightly, and she repeated the word but drew it out— "Oooohhhh"—like she'd finally gotten the joke someone had told moments ago.

"What?" Sarah crossed her arms over her chest and waited. It was the only way she knew to deal with her mother when she was being the "know it all."

"Nothing," she said, and she took Sarah's arm and led her back down the hallway into her own bedroom. When she pushed lightly, Sarah fell back on her mother's bed and crossed her arms behind her head, prepared to wait her out.

Her mother's room was an explosion of colors. Where the hallway could pass as moderately organized, her mother's rooms were complete chaos in Sarah's mind. Each wall was painted a different bright color. Brightly colored beads, which usually hung on her mother's canopy, had been tied up to each of the posts. There were more of her paintings hanging on the walls and even more stacked against the walls.

Her mother had found an oversized purple sofa years ago. It had taken three of her cousin's friends to carry the beast up the back stairs and place it in its final resting spot under the bay windows. Her mother's dresser looked like it had come directly off the cheap furniture truck, yet Sarah knew it was well over thirty years old and still looked new.

Incense burned constantly when her mother was home, causing the rooms to be slightly smoky.

"I like him," her mother said, dropping both towels as she stood in front of her closet naked, looking for another colorful outfit to wear that day.

"I'm sure Ben will be happy to hear that." Sarah shifted on the bed, getting more comfortable since she knew it took her mother a while to pick out an outfit.

Sure enough, her mother started tossing clothes onto the bed, trying desperately to pick something. Sarah had asked her once why it took so long. Her mother's reply was that when she came across the right outfit, she would know. This was one of the main reasons Sarah never second-guessed her clothing each day.

Crystal turned to her and frowned. Sarah hated that look since she knew it was identical to the one she often had. Her mother wasn't really a frowning type of person. For almost ninety percent of her life, she could only remember her smiling.

"Why are you trying to deny what's between the two of you?"

Sarah rolled her eyes. "Next you're going to tell me you saw this all happening in my charts…"

"Not this." Her mother's frown increased until she turned her back on her.

"What then?" Sarah hated being curious, but for most of her life, her mother's "charts" had been somewhat accurate. Sarah figured early on that it never hurt to listen to her mother's advice. After all, the woman was, despite the content of the wares, a very successful business owner.

And she'd been lucky enough to find and fall in love with her soul mate early on in life, even if he had died too early. Most people never get to experience the kind of love her parents had, no matter how fleeting.

"That's not important. The important thing is…"—her mother pulled out a bright yellow dress, nodded, then slipped it over her body sans any undergarments— "how you feel about him."

She turned towards Sarah and Sarah wondered why her mother was still single. They could pass for sisters and, even with the hints of laugh lines around her mother's eyes, she couldn't deny that the woman was beautiful.

"I'm not sure how I feel about him yet. He's here to do a job. One that I had hoped would be mine one day. Yet…" Sarah sat up, propping her body up with her elbows. "He's different than I'd expected." Her eyes narrowed as she glanced out her mother's window, thinking.

When she felt the bed shift, she glanced over to see her mother sit next to her. When she reached out and took her hand, Sarah smiled.

"Did I ever tell you about the first time I met your father?"

"Yes, many times. You ran into him on the beach at night."

"No." Crystal smiled. "That was the first time I knew I loved your father. We had met weeks before that." Crystal shifted, wrapping her arms around Sarah so they leaned against her headboard.

"I thought…" Sarah shook her head. "No, tell me." She settled back, prepared to hear how her parents had met.

"Well, back then I was working at a resort as a waitress." Sarah nodded her head, not wanting to interrupt her mother's story. "Your father was sent by his parents to see if the resort was something they wanted to save. Apparently, back then, it wasn't as profitable as it could be and they were thinking of selling."

Sarah felt her heart skip. She'd known that her father had been sent to East Haven for that purpose, but each time she heard it, she ached.

"What happened?" Her mother was running her fingers through her hair, something she'd always done when holding her close. It not only soothed her but reassured her that she was loved.

"Well, the first morning Jon was there, I was on shift. I'd just arrived on the ferry that morning and hadn't heard yet that the boss's son was on the island. So, I set off to work, taking orders, delivering food, and busing tables." She glanced down at Sarah. "You know how it is." Sarah nodded. "By the end of the morning rush, I was covered in a layer of sweat and my apron had eggs down the front since there had been a rather large group of children present. They were having the Anderson's yearly reunion that week." Sarah groaned and closed her eyes.

"I know what you mean." She knew the large wealthy family that took over the entire island for a week and a half each year. Children ran unsupervised, teens broke things or, even once, burned things, and the parents were too busy squabbling about who would inherit the next big chunk of money to care what anyone else thought about them.

"Anyway, in walks your father. I thought he was a potential beau for one of the Anderson daughters. So, naturally, I ignored him completely and went about my business. Well, your father was having none of that. He actually followed me into the back serving hall and cornered me, demanding to know my name." Sarah felt her mother's chest rise and fall as she chuckled.

"What did you do?" Sarah bit her bottom lip, waiting.

"I slapped him," her mother said, shocking her. Sarah sat up, her eyes going wide.

"You what?"

Crystal dipped her chin, her smile going big. "Actually, it was more of a right cross. Your grandfather demanded that both of his daughters could protect ourselves, so he enrolled us in self-defense classes."

She couldn't stop the smile from her own lips. Her grandfather Holley had not only demanded Sarah take the same self-defense classes but had made her cousin Rowan do so, as well.

"What did dad do?" She leaned back, looking at her mother as she leaned against the headboard.

"He smiled."

"And?"

"That was it. Just smiled back at me."

Sarah shook her head, not understanding.

"I turned on my heels and rushed into the kitchen. I was going on about how some arrogant bastard had tried to hit on me when Tom rushed in and told me who he was. Naturally, he forced me to go up to Jon's rooms to apologize."

"What happened then?"

"We fell in love," Crystal said, her eyes closing as tears fell down her cheeks. Sarah pulled her mother towards her and wrapped her arms around her.

CHAPTER 10

*H*is legs burned as he followed Sarah. He'd expected to spend a day in town, shopping or driving around as she pointed out the views, not hiking up an almost vertical trail.

After enjoying a wonderful homemade breakfast, including hot bread from the oven, Sarah had grabbed a large blue backpack and headed out in the front seat of a beat-up pickup truck.

"It's Rowan's, but he won't mind. He has keys to my car just in case," she'd said, backing out of the spot across the street. He'd gotten a better look at the homes around hers in the daylight. The place that sat directly across from hers was half its size. Still, the two-story building was impressive. It had been painted a more moderate taupe color but had a bright blue door and a swing on the front porch.

Sarah had driven quickly through town until they had reached the outskirts and then had turned off on another road and driven for over thirty minutes. She talked the entire way about the town of Silver Cove and the people in it, never once talking about East Haven or her job.

He listened and asked questions when there was a slight break in the conversation. She asked him more about his family, and he gave short and quick answers.

Finally, she pulled off into a dirt parking lot and pulled out her backpack. He followed her as she headed out on Summit Trail. The path had started at a nice slope, but shortly after the old yellow steel bridge, the trail had taken a steeper turn.

They had passed what appeared to be a historic homestead site, but Sarah hadn't stopped, so he couldn't check out the markers to find out what had transpired at the location.

He loved history. It had been one of his favorite classes in school. He knew all the important sites near where he lived and the dates of significant events. He found it odd that most people passed by street after street in Boston without knowing what their ancestors had done there long before them.

"Where are we going?" he finally managed once they reached a clearing. It wasn't as if he was breathless, just… winded.

"You'll see," she said over her shoulder. She appeared to be unfazed by the steepness or the briskness of their walk. So, naturally, he stepped up his game.

When they reached the end of the path, he became breathless for an altogether different reason. The pathway opened up to a large flat boulder that overlooked miles and miles of treetops. Off in the distance, he could make out a small ranch they had passed. Its bright red barn and crisp white fence looked like something out of a puzzle he'd put together when he'd been a child.

There were almost a dozen people on the stone face, enjoying the warm sun and the view.

Sarah walked closer to the cliff's edge and set her bag down. Her hand came up to shield the sun as she glanced around and took several deep breaths. When she turned to him, her lips curved up.

"You're supposed to be enjoying the view." She nodded towards the scenery.

He took two steps closer to her and wrapped his arms around her waist. "Who says I'm not?"

They stood there holding each other for a few moments until finally, he stepped back. "Now, are you going to tell me why we're here?" He glanced around.

"This isn't reason enough?" She motioned to the view.

"I mean, why here and not shopping in town?"

Sarah snickered and sat down next to her bag. She pulled out a bottled water and handed him one. "I'm not the shopping type."

His eyebrows rose as he folded his body down next to hers. Her elbows were resting lightly on her knees and, for the first time, he looked at what she was wearing: worn jeans, which had obviously seen many washes, and a red and black flannel shirt with a black tank top underneath. The sleeves were rolled up to the elbows since it had been a rather warm hike up the hill. Her hiking boots looked even more worn than her jeans did.

"You really like this?" He glanced around, taking in the sites as he drank the water she'd given him.

"Don't you?" She looked at him through the sides of her eyes.

"Sure, but I've never met a woman that likes hiking." He smiled. "And one that can whoop my ass on such a steep incline."

Her laughter echoed off the stone. "Rowan and I used to race one another up the trail."

"I bet you always won."

She turned her shoulders towards him. "Not always." He could see the love for her cousin in her eyes.

"You're lucky to have such a wonderful family."

He hadn't meant to turn the conversation, but when her eyes turned sad, he looked off towards the red barn.

"I imagine that farm is the most photographed thing around." He rested his elbows on his knees and tried to relax.

"It's been featured in books, calendars, magazines, and even on several puzzles," she said, taking his empty water bottle and putting them both back into her pack.

"I knew I'd seen it before."

"On a book?" she asked.

"No, a puzzle." He leaned back on his elbows.

"Do you like puzzles?" she asked.

"Don't you?"

She shook her head and leaned back on her backpack. "Not particularly. I like to see the whole picture before I spend any energy on something."

He realized they weren't talking about a game that had hundreds of pieces, anymore.

"Isn't that the whole point, to see something new unfold before your eyes?" He reached over and started running his hand down her arm. "Kind of like starting a new relationship and slowly discovering who it is you're with."

She sat up and just looked at him until finally he chuckled and said, "What?"

"You're a romantic. I would never have guessed it."

This time it was his laughter that bounced off the rocks. "Isn't everyone?"

"Sure, I mean, at least a little. Otherwise, our race would probably be doomed. But who would have guessed that underneath the business suit, you would have a heart of mush," she joked as she leaned back down and relaxed.

"After meeting your mother, I would have thought that you would be more of a romantic yourself."

"Maybe I decided long ago to take an opposite road than Crystal did." He watched her bite her bottom lip.

"Why?" He reached out and took her hand and played with a silver ring on one of her fingers. Her chest rose and fell as she thought about her answer.

"Too many reasons to list. You're just visiting Silver Cove. You weren't raised here, forced to deal with spiteful people who don't like someone who's a little different."

"You see enough of it in the city still."

"I suppose. But all you need to do is turn the corner to escape." She looked out to the treetops. "There aren't a lot of places to hide in Silver Cove."

"Is this one of those places?" he asked her softly.

Her mind revisited the many times she and Rowan had escaped up here as teens. Even with the drive, it was one of their most cherished hangouts. They had spent even more time there after Lori's death, camping out as much as they could. But then Rowan had moved away to college and, feeling abandoned, she'd started spending most of her days off on the island instead.

"Yes." She leaned up and looked out over the vastness. "Everyone thinks it's the most beautiful in the fall when the leaves are changing."

"Isn't it?"

"It's lovely." She crossed her arms over her knees and tilted her head as her eyes closed, remembering. "But the best time is after a fresh snowfall. You can start a campfire up here and watch the stars come out after the clouds clear."

"See, you are a romantic." He reached over and took her hand in his. When he raised it up to his lips and gently kissed the underside of her wrist, she felt her heart skip.

The conversation turned lighter and they chatted about Boston and how life in a big city was different than the country. People around them came and went and before long, she felt her stomach growl. Standing up, she dusted off her jeans and held her hand out for him.

"Come on. How about we go enjoy some of the greasiest burgers around?"

"I've got a strong stomach." He stood up and wrapped his arms around her hips and held her tight. "We all escape in our own ways." He glanced around, over her shoulder. "I have to say; your escaping spot is a lot better than any I've ever had." Then he dipped his head down and brushed his lips across hers.

She'd been trying to convince herself to keep her distance from him, but when he acted like that, how was she supposed to refuse him? Even her body betrayed her plans as she melted in his arms and her lips heated under his.

She hadn't realized there was a bite to the air until he released her and her body missed his warmth. She leaned down to pick up her pack, only to have him beat her to the task.

"Did you and your cousin always race back down?"

She smiled. "That's something he never could beat me at."

"Then I won't have to give you a head start," he joked as they walked to the edge of the large stone. "Ready?" He glanced at her as he threw her backpack over his shoulders.

Giving him a quick nod, she broke into a quick run as she heard him follow. When she made it to the halfway mark, she allowed him to gain ground, even letting him pass her. He fell right into her trap.

When he reached the bottom, he was gasping for air and frowning at her as she leaned casually against the wood fence in front of the truck.

"You cheated," he accused her as he leaned down and took a few deep breaths.

Her eyebrows went up. "I never cheat." She stood up and took her pack from him, pulling out two bottles of water and handing him one. He gulped it down much more quickly than he had the one at the top of the hill. She drank more slowly.

"There has to be a shortcut," he said finally after catching his breath.

"No one ever said you had to use the same path coming down."

"Next time," he promised. "Does your cousin know you cheat?"

She laughed as she opened the truck door. "Who do you think taught me?"

The drive back into town seemed quicker. She had allowed herself to get hungrier than she'd planned, and her foot was a little heavy on the pedal. She made it to Roy's Diner in record time.

"I'm starved," Ben said, shutting his door. "And, if the food is as good as it smells, I'll be in heaven." He reached over and casually took her hand as they walked into the old-time diner.

Roy's had been around long before she'd been born. Her parents had often come here and she remembered sitting in the booth in the corner with both of them smiling and laughing together.

That, along with almost a hundred other wonderful memories, made Roy's her third favorite place in Silver Cove.

As they walked in, the wonderful smells hit them both. She closed her eyes and took a deep breath, enjoying it along with the sounds of a busy diner under the blare of the King of Rock-n-Roll playing from the jukebox.

The old red bar stools could stand to be reupholstered, as could some of the booth seats, but everything else gleamed. The black-and-white checkered tile floors had recently been replaced. Old pictures of movie stars and music legends hung on the walls.

"Hey, Sarah, sit anywhere you want," Krystle, one of the longest-running employees of the diner, said as she carried a large tray above her shoulder. She paused for a moment and winked at Sarah after getting a look at Ben holding her hand.

"Oh, looks like you've got some gossip to tell," she said before hurrying off to deliver the food.

When she heard Ben chuckle next to her, she dropped his hand and made her way towards her favorite corner booth.

"So, what's good to eat here?" Ben asked, glancing down at the menu she'd handed him from behind the salt and pepper. Since she knew it by heart, she hadn't even pulled one out for herself.

Instead, she took the time to glance around. There were several people she recognized, some from school, others from just around town. So far, there wasn't anyone she was trying to avoid. She always did this when she visited town. First, she would scan and see if there were potential problem makers, then she would do everything in her power to avoid a conflict.

"Everything. If you like meatloaf, they have the best around. Their steaks are the best in the state, the fried chicken the best in county, and the burgers…" She closed her eyes and groaned out in delight. "The best in the world."

He laughed. "Burgers it is then." He set his menu down and looked at her.

"We've been avoiding one topic today."

Her eye moved up to his. "What would that be?" For some reason, her heart skipped.

"Why are you staying around here?"

She blinked a few times. His question had thrown her off for a moment. He leaned back and looked at her, and then he continued.

"You're obviously very good at what you do. There isn't one employee who doesn't speak very highly of you.

Since you've been managing the resort, profits are up, costs are down, and…" He leaned closer, keeping his eyes on her. "The place has been solidly booked. Even during the off-season."

She felt a little of the pressure leave her chest. "Then why are you here?"

She saw something cross his eyes before he leaned away. Just then Krystle walked over to their table with a large chocolate mint shake.

"Here you go, sweetie." Krystle smiled down at her. "What'll you have, sexy?" She glanced over at Ben. Sarah could have sworn the older woman's smile doubled.

"That looks good." Ben nodded towards her milkshake.

Krystle wrote it down on her notepad. "Your usual?" she asked Sarah.

"Yes, make it two," she added, then took a sip of her shake and smiled. "Like I always say, your shakes are the best in the universe. When are you going to come work at the resort?"

Krystle laughed. "When they build a bridge. I don't fly or go on a boat. I keep my feet planted firmly on the ground." Krystle leaned closer to her and whispered loud enough for Ben to hear. "Looks like you've been up in the clouds yourself." She nodded towards Ben and then disappeared towards the back to enter their order.

"I like her," Ben said between laughs.

"Who doesn't?"

Just then the bell above the door chimed and Sarah glanced over in time to see Joe and Angie walk in the door together. A deep frown formed on her lips as she quickly glanced away.

Memories of being teased surfaced, as did anger at the fact that, for some reason, it still hurt her, even though she was more successful than either of them would ever be. When it came to her past, the present didn't matter.

"What?" Ben said, reaching over and taking her hand. "Are you okay?"

"Yes." She glanced out the large windows and noticed dark clouds coming in off the bluff. "Looks like we'll have rain tonight."

"Sarah." Ben leaned closer. "Don't think I didn't see what just happened. Talk to me."

She shook her head and rolled her eyes. "It's in the past."

"Those two?" He nodded towards the couple who were now sitting at the bar area, ordering their meal.

"Them, and a class full of others just like them."

"Surely there must have been one person, besides Rowan."

Sarah shook her head. "One summer there was a girl named Melissa. But she moved away. Her father was in the military."

"There wasn't anyone else?" He squeezed her hand lightly.

"Krystle, Tom, Rodney…" She started to list.

"No one your age?" he broke in.

"I didn't need friends."

"Everyone needs friends."

"I have them now. Lilith, Heather…"

"Work friends."

"They're more than just my work friends," she started to argue, only to have him pull on her hand until she leaned closer.

"I'm still in almost daily contact with my best friend from grade school. Mike and I have been through thick and thin. We grew up together, got drunk for the first time together, and in high school lost our virginity to the Baker sisters on the same night. We even went away to the same college together."

"Where is he now?" She hadn't realized it, but she was smiling as she listened to him talk about his friend. His eyes were full of laughter when he talked about Mike, making her wish she could meet the man, herself. But, if Ben made up his mind to take the job, she would most likely never see him again, since she'd made up her mind to move out of Silver Cove for good.

CHAPTER 11

By the time Sarah parked the truck in front of the house, the rain was coming down in buckets. The sound the water made on the top of the old truck was the most soothing sound he'd ever heard. Reaching over, he took Sarah's hand to stop her from racing from the warmth inside the vehicle.

"Let's wait it out a bit," he suggested, pulling her across the wide seat, towards him. He felt her tense for a moment, but when his arms wrapped around her, she relaxed. The sun had disappeared behind the clouds, casting a darkness over the town so that the streetlights came on early. Most likely, the sun wouldn't make another appearance before it sank below the hills that night.

"Thanks for today," he said, close to her lips. "I can honestly say it was the most unexpected, pleasure-filled day I've had in a long time."

Her smile was quick. He loved the way a dimple played at the corner of her lips. Reaching up, he brushed his finger over the spot and then watched as her lips dipped down into a frown.

"Ben, I'm not sure…" Now there was a slight crease between her eyebrows, so his finger trailed up until he brushed the spot softly. "It's just… I…things can't get complicated between us."

"Sarah." He felt his chest bursting as he held in his emotions. "It's already too late for that." Her lips were soft and warm under his. For a moment, her fingers went to his shoulders as if she were going to push him away, but instead, her nails dug in.

He pushed her jacket off her shoulders, and when she didn't stop him, proceeded to move his hands under her shirt until he could feel her warm skin against his palms. A low moan escaped her lips, causing him to enter an almost giddy state.

When she moved quickly over him, trapping his hips tight against the insides of her thighs, he jolted with need. Now it was he who moaned as she used her hips to grind into his length. He felt his eyes almost cross, so he closed them and roamed his hands over every inch of her he could.

He felt her heartbeat under his fingertips, tasted the sweet spot under her ears, and felt it kick there too. She tasted like a warm spring day and felt even better.

He wasn't sure if he had the strength to stop if she asked it of him. He'd never been this challenged before, had never been pushed this far, this fast.

His fingers brushed up against the top of her jeans, and he dipped a finger under and felt her melt even more against him. Moving quickly, he reversed their positions until she was lying flat on the long soft bench. One of her legs was hiked over his hip, the other trapped under him.

It took only a quick tug to have her jeans riding low over her hips. He released her lips from his and traveled down to the spot he'd exposed under her shirt so he could enjoy the warmth and the softness there.

Her fingers gripped his hair, tugging him, holding him where she wanted him most. Then, when he traveled down to the dip of her belly button, he felt her hips sway and her legs shake.

His fingers roamed down slowly, gently pulling aside her simple pink cotton panties until he exposed her completely to his view. When he brushed his fingers over her, her hips jumped off the bench.

"Easy," he chuckled, watching her eyes zero in on his.

"Ben," she started, but he just shushed her and ran his finger over her exposed flesh once more. When he did, she closed her eyes with pleasure. Her head tilted back and her fingers dug into the cushion of the bench.

As he dipped a finger into her, he heard a low sound come from deep within her chest. When his eyes moved back to hers, he realized it was him that was making the noise.

He wanted her. Wanted to rip his jeans down and embed himself within her as fast as he could. Taking her quickly, selfishly, wholly. But he wasn't that kind of a lover. Had never been. Instead, he gentled his fingers as his eyes closed so he could gain some sort of control.

When he opened his eyes again, he looked down at her. Her jeans hung very low around her knees, but she was still wearing those hiking boots, and there was a mile of laces to deal with. He chose not to deal with them and leave her jeans where they were. Besides, now she was trapped under him, exactly where he wanted her.

He bent down, scooting to the very end of the bench, as he dipped his head and ran his tongue over her swollen skin. Her hips jerked under him, so he spread his hand out over her stomach, holding her down so he could further explore her rich, honey tastes.

"Ben, I can't… I'm…"

"Let go. Give me what I want," he growled next to her skin. Her fingers dug into his hair, holding him as she gave him everything she had.

"Okay, I can mark that off my list of to-dos," she joked as they removed their wet jackets in the back hallway.

"Hmm?" Ben stopped shaking his coat to look at her.

"That." She jerked her head back to where she'd parked Rowan's truck. Then her mind spun. They had just… in Rowan's truck! She felt her cheeks begin to burn, only to be shaken out of her embarrassment when she heard Ben chuckling.

"Surely you've done… that… in a car before?"

She hung her jacket up and started to walk down the hallway into the kitchen without answering him. His hand on her arm stopped her just inside the room.

"Really?" His smile was growing bigger, no doubt causing her to turn even redder. "Wow, I'm honored that I'm your first in-car experience."

She chuckled at his words. "Kind of like an in-flight movie?"

He smiled as he pulled her closer. "If you want… that could be a pre—"

Just then the kitchen door burst open and her mother walked in with a man. A very tall, tan, man around her own age.

Her arms dropped quickly, and she took a step back.

"Crystal," she said, feeling her red face turn a little pale. "Joe." Her voice was icy as his name left her lips.

"Oh, you are here," Crystal said, walking to the fridge and pulling out a bottled water. "We were just doing some yoga. Joe here is the best instructor."

"If you can call him that," Sarah said under her breath.

"What was that dear?" Her mother's head popped out from the fridge.

"We were just heading upstairs," she lied, seeing Joe's eyes narrow slightly.

"Oh, well, I thought we could all hang…"

"Can't," she said quickly, taking Ben's hand and pulling him towards the stairs.

"Oh, well, okay. We're probably going to head out and grab some food."

"Don't wait up for us," Joe added, and his perfect smile made Sarah wish she could bash it in.

"Whoa, whoa," Ben said, stopping her as she slammed the door to her room shut. "What was that about?"

She'd been so upset; she'd dragged him up the two flights of stairs into her own rooms without knowing it. "Sorry." She stepped back from him and started pacing the floor. To calm herself down, her eyes moved around her space.

Her rooms were big enough that she had space to pace. Her bedroom was the same size as his downstairs, but the hallway between it and the room across the way were enclosed and the two rooms were connected, opening up to one another with a high archway. The bathroom door was in between the two areas. Sarah had decorated the other area as a TV and sitting area. She had a small desk that held her laptop and even had a table for eating.

Here, her personality showed in the art she'd hung on the walls and the colors she'd painted them—light colors, taupes, and creams, with a hint of bright teal here and there. She'd loved her space since she'd redecorated the first summer after she'd started working at the resort full time.

"Mind telling me what that was all about?" Ben came up behind her and took her shoulders gently to stop her pacing.

She turned in his arms, keeping her shoulders stiff. "That man. I don't know why my mother doesn't see right through his act. She's normally really good at reading people's auras—her words, not mine."

His eyebrows rose slightly. "Have you talked to her about how you feel about him?"

She pushed away from him and walked over to her window. The view was the same as his, and even though it was dark and raining out, her mind could still see the flowers and trees below in the garden.

"No, I didn't want to…"

His hands came down once more lightly on her shoulders. "What has he done to cause so much animosity in you?"

"The usual. Ever since my father, my mother's taste in men has gone extremely downhill."

"How?"

"The men are scum." She lifted her shoulders and when they relaxed a little, she realized his fingers were gently massaging them. It felt wonderful and her eyes slid closed for a moment as she felt herself let go even more.

"Maybe she's afraid?"

She turned towards him. "Afraid? Of what?"

She stood still as he wrapped his arms around her and pulled her a step closer. "The same thing you are. Allowing herself to fall too deep. Your mothers found a way of keeping herself distant, by picking men that could never happen with."

In that moment, something shifted in Sarah's heart, causing a pain to settle over the spot. It was like the missing piece of her mother's puzzle finally settled into place.

"I never…" She felt a tear slip down her face. He reached up with a finger and softly wiped it away with his thumb. She leaned into him and wrapped her arms around him, holding on as the tears flowed.

His fingers tangled in her hair, gently stroking it as he comforted her.

"It only makes me love her even more. Why does she do things like this?" She felt him chuckle and smiled. "I really hate that guy."

He pulled back and looked down at her. "What has he done?"

She linked her fingers behind his back. "He's hit on me. Several times when my mother wasn't around."

She felt Ben shake slightly. "Now I hate the man." She almost laughed at the visible anger she saw in his eyes.

"He's quite harmless. Just full of himself, that's all."

"Still." He started to take a step back, but her arms

locked around him as she smiled. "What? Are you going to go downstairs and defend me?"

His dark eyes met hers. "I'm thinking about it." But his arms went back around her.

"I'd rather you stay up here. With me," she added.

Just as he leaned down to rub his lips over hers, his phone chimed in his pocket.

"Sorry," he mumbled and pulled the phone out. He frowned as he glanced down at the screen. "I need to take this." He nodded towards her door as he clicked on the phone and stepped out.

She stood there, desperately wishing her walls weren't so thick, so she could hear his conversation. Creeping closer, she did hear one phase, which caused her skin to crawl. Thoughts about why it wasn't a good idea to get involved with Benjamin Rothschild surfaced all over again.

She turned on her heels and, crossing her arms over her chest, and fought the urge to throw something solid at his head when he stepped back into the room.

She heard her door open and close but didn't allow him enough time to walk across and place his hands on her again.

"Is Elite selling East Haven?" She knew there was a bite to her tone, but at this point, she didn't care.

"What?" She saw the look in his eyes before he had time to mask it.

"Why come here? To toy with us? Why did Elite send you here?" She hadn't realized she'd been shouting until her words echoed in her rooms.

"I'm not at liberty—"

Taking a deep breath, she dropped her arms to her

sides. "I think it's best you leave," she broke in, not wanting to hear the same line of why he couldn't divulge his job or the intentions of the company they both worked for.

"Oookay," he said as he held his hands out to her. "Sarah," he started.

"Don't." She held her hands up, stopping him. "We both knew this wasn't going to go anywhere. Not with the job and Elite between us. It's too big of a wall." She shook her head, hoping the tears would wait until after he'd left. "Just go. I'll drive you back to East Haven tomorrow morning. You can spend the rest of the week there."

"I don't want—"

Her chin when up, causing his words to stop.

"If that's what you want."

"Goodnight." She turned back towards her window and, as she watched the rain fall, she listened carefully as he left her rooms. She could hear him descend the staircase since there were boards that creaked, but after that, the house remained silent.

She'd been a fool! Closing her eyes, she allowed the tears to finally slip down her face. Looking at it, her mother's plan was beginning to look solid enough. If you never put your heart out there, there was no chance of it getting hurt. Like hers hurt now.

She crawled under the blankets still fully clothed and cried herself to sleep.

CHAPTER 12

The next morning Ben sat next to Sarah as she drove her car back towards the docks. He could tell she was upset and couldn't blame her. But he had a job to do and he was a man of his word. His boss didn't want Sarah to know what his plans were, and he figured there must be a good reason. Besides, breaking the trust of the man signing his paychecks wouldn't be good for his career.

So, he sat silently as she drove him back to the ferry. Jerry was already docked, standing in the sunshine waiting for them. Instead of pulling her car onto the flatbed of the boat, she stopped on the edge of the dock and waved towards Jerry.

"I hope you don't mind, but I've got a few things to take care of this morning." She glanced over at him.

"No, of course." He reached for his bag, only to stop. "Sarah, I'm not keeping this from you because I want to. I'm under strict orders to—"

"From whom?" she interrupted.

"My boss."

"Who is?" She waited, but all he could do was shake his head.

"The same company you work for."

"Yes, but—"

"Listen, I understand you have questions. All I can promise you is that by this time next month, you'll have those answers."

"I may not be here then."

His heart skipped. "Why? Where are you—?"

"Ben, we both know that if Elite chooses to promote another person to manager, it would be better for me to move on." Her fingers tightened on her steering wheel. "I had hoped… someday…" She shook her head. "I can't wait around for something that's never going to happen."

"Don't make any rash decisions." He turned to her, taking her hands in his. She stiffened, but he pulled her closer. "Please, promise me that you will wait to make any choices until I come back."

"So, you will be back?" Her eyes teared up and he wished more than anything he could take the pain he saw behind those blue eyes away.

He nodded slowly. "I should be back within the month."

Her shoulders jerked as she pushed him away. "I can't make any promises." She turned her eyes away.

"Just until I get back," he begged and held his breath until finally, she nodded her head.

"I won't abandon East Haven like that," she finally said.

He didn't know what that meant, but he took her

promise and felt a little relieved. "I'll see you later this week when you come back?"

She bobbed her head abruptly, and he felt a little better.

"Until then," he promised, hopping out of her car before she could change her mind.

"What did you do to piss her off?" Jerry joked as they started to pull away from the dock.

"My job." He frowned as he watched the dust settle from her car on the road. "Just my job."

He settled back into the same room. He hadn't been surprised when Lilith informed him that Sarah had arranged for him to stay the remainder of the week already.

As he settled in for a few peaceful days of quiet, he kept playing the day before in his mind.

It had, without a doubt, been one of the best days of his life. Not that his life had been crap, but he'd never experienced such a feeling of freedom before. He was on the brink of turning twenty-eight and in the last day, he'd realized, to his shock, that he didn't even know himself.

He liked being outdoors, but now he was realizing that he really liked being in the country. Even more, it was becoming apparent to him that he'd been living in a haze the last few years, ever since he'd moved up the ladder at Elite.

He was nothing more than a go-to-guy and, to his horror, he realized he hated his job. Looking back over the past few months, he couldn't point out one day, one freaking day, that stood out in his mind. Every day had become just like the one before. Mindless. Pointless.

He looked around the room and decided he needed a long walk. Pulling on his jacket again, he set out, almost bumping into Lilith, who had been standing just outside his doorway.

"Sorry," she whispered, trying to move aside.

"Can I help you with something?" he asked, dropping his hands from her shoulders after making sure she wasn't going to tip over.

"Um." She looked around. "I was just…" Her eyes moved everywhere, but she kept avoiding his face.

"Eavesdropping?" He chortled.

"I'm just curious," Lilith begged. "Honest, she didn't ask me to or anything." He watched as the woman's face turned a light shade of pink.

"Easy." He smiled and took her shoulders, steering her into his room. "Why don't you sit down and tell me everything."

"Everything?" She bit her bottom lip.

"Well, whatever you want to spill." He pulled the desk chair out and turned it around to sit across from her. "So, are you wondering why I'm back so soon?"

Her head wobbled. "No, Sarah called me early this morning, when she asked me to get the room ready for you."

"So?" He hinted for her to start talking.

"Well, since you two left for the mainland, everyone's been talking."

"And?" Once more he tried to keep her talking.

"You're not here for us, are you?" She played with the hem of her shirt in a nervous manner. "I mean, you're not here to see if you want Sarah's job. You're here for her."

He tilted his head, not knowing what to say, knowing he couldn't say anything. Lilith's eyes moved up to his and held them trapped.

"I knew it. I just knew it." Her voice rose slightly. "You're here to see if she's qualified."

He leaned back and crossed his arms over his chest. Still not saying anything.

"Well?"

"I can neither confirm nor deny…"

Lilith shocked him by letting out a quick squeal and jumping up and down on the bed. "Well?" She finally said once she calmed down. "You don't have to tell me what decision you came to." She smiled over at him. "After all, Sarah is the best thing that's ever happened to East Haven." Lilith jumped up, gave him a quick hug, and rushed for the door.

"Lilith." She stopped at the door, one hand on the handle. "I can't tell you how important it is that Sarah not find out. If she did, it would mean both of our jobs."

Her smile fell away slightly. "Seriously?"

His head dipped quickly. "Direct orders from the highest source in Elite Resorts. That's why Sarah got mad and why I'm staying here all week by myself."

Lilith's lips turned downward in a frown. "Maybe I can help you out." His eyebrows moved upward in question. Lilith's smile was back. "Just leave it all to me." Her smile grew. "I'll take care of everything," she said before rushing out of the room without another word.

He was too restless to stay cooped up in the room, especially since he now questioned what mysterious plans Lilith had. He didn't know her very well but guessed she had a serious mischievous streak in her.

So, he headed out once more for a long walk around the island.

He passed a few employees as he walked. Heather was

getting the back deck ready for what looked like a wedding party. Rodney was in the gardens, pruning back some of the new growth.

The rain the evening before made all of the paths look clean and new. He noticed small flower buds growing on several of the rose bushes in the gardens and imagined what the place would look like in full bloom.

He continued down the pathway and somehow ended up on the beach. Deciding he wasn't in the mood for a walk anymore, he sat in the soft sand and brooded about what his life was going to be like once he returned to Boston. How was he going to be happy without Sarah?

Sarah stood over Lilith's bed two days later, frowning down at her friend. "You should go to the ER with a temperature this high." She looked worriedly down at the thermometer.

"No," Lilith said, coughing. "I'll be fine. I just need a few days of rest." Lilith shivered, so Sarah reached down and pulled the blankets up higher. She brushed a hand down her face and jumped at the warmth.

"You're burning up." She stood up to make a phone call to a doctor, only to be stopped by Lilith.

"Sarah, really. It's just the flu. I just need some rest. I'm really sorry you had to come work on your week off."

"Don't be." Sarah reached over and took her friend's warm hand. "I'd do anything for your silly face."

Lilith's chuckle turned into a cough.

"That's it; I'm heading downstairs to have Adam make up some of that smelly stuff that helped Ben." Just mentioning his name caused her heart to hurt. Ben. She hadn't thought about him. Or the fact that she was now, once more, stuck on the island with him. Shaking her head slightly, she decided to think about that later. She knew, better than anyone else, there were ways to avoid a person on the small island.

"No!" Lilith begged. "I won't eat it. After what that man did to me." Her friend started to sit up but stopped when Sarah pushed her back down.

"You'll eat every bite of it."

"He might poison it," Lilith said halfheartedly, causing Sarah to smile.

"He wouldn't dare. Besides, I'm really under the impression that he likes you. I think it's how the French men show interest."

"How? By being annoying?"

Sarah laughed and quickly hugged her friend's warm body. "Rest. I'll bring up the soup when I can. Do you need anything else?"

Lilith shook her head and closed her eyes. "Just some sleep. I'm really light-headed."

Sarah started to walk out but stopped when Lilith called her name.

"Thank you for coming back." Her friend smiled over at her.

"Rest," Sarah demanded, and then she left to head to the kitchen to have Adam make his family recipe.

As she walked back to the main building, she thought of a plan to keep away from Ben until Monday. She was so preoccupied with the details; she didn't see him strolling towards her until it was too late.

"What are you doing back here so early?"

"Lilith…" She started to explain, only to see his eyes heat.

"What did she tell you?" he demanded.

"Nothing…" She frowned. "She's sick."

"Oh. Ooohhh." He inclined his head and she watched as his eyes softened.

"What does she know that you don't want her telling me?" She crossed her arms over her chest.

"Nothing." He coughed. "It's just, I… um… broke a chair."

"You… broke a chair?"

"Yeah, I was… In my room. I was…" His eyes moved around, and she couldn't quite tell if he was embarrassed or searching for something to say. "I was hanging my swim shorts on the shower rod and… snap. The leg broke. Lilith saw it and…"

"You broke a chair and you didn't want Lilith telling me about it?"

"Yup." He took her arm and started walking towards the back door. "So, you're here because Lilith is sick?"

She stopped just outside the back door and looked up at him. "I'll be filling in for her for a few days until she's back on her feet."

He glanced towards the building that housed all the employee's rooms. "Should I stop by and visit her?"

"No, she's getting some rest. I'm about to send up a bowl of Adam's special family recipe that helped you so much."

"Good." He smiled, taking her shoulders once more. "I was hoping you'd change your mind and come back early—"

"Ben, nothing has changed between us. I have a job to

do, and so do you." She reached for the back door, but his hand on hers stopped her.

"Sarah, I'm not going to make excuses for not telling you what Elite's plans are since it's not my place, but I will say this. What we had was personal and if you can't see that this…"—he motioned between them— "has nothing to do with Elite or with East Haven, then maybe there wasn't anything, to begin with."

He was right. She'd been telling herself the same thing the last two days as she brooded up in her rooms.

Her feelings for him had nothing to do with Elite or the fact that he was there to take her life-long dream job.

"Meet me tonight." He moved a step closer to her. "On the beach."

She felt her heart soften a little at the desperation in his voice. Then, the rest of her reservations drop away.

"I won't get done with the party until around ten."

"Then I'll see you there at ten thirty?"

She dipped her head slightly. "I'll bring the dessert this time," she said before rushing into the building. Once inside, she rested her shoulders against the door and took several cleansing breaths. What had she just promised?

Her face heated as she closed her eyes. She knew what she'd said. And part of her really meant it. She wanted him. At least once before he left for good. Or became her boss.

"Is everything alright?" Adam asked. When she looked, the man had stopped in the middle of his kitchen and was looking at her with a concerned stare.

"Yes. No. Lilith is sick. That's why I'm back so soon."

She saw concern flood his blue eyes. "Oui, I will start

on the broth now." He moved to set down the pan he'd been working on.

"No, keep working on the dinner. Lilith can wait until after supper. However, you might have to get someone else to deliver it up to her room since Heather and I will be busy with the wedding."

"Oui." He nodded briskly. "I will take care of it myself."

Sarah hid a slight smile as she made her way up to her office. She was sure Lilith was going to kill her for sending Adam to her room while she was feeling and looking so bad. But she'd seen his eyes fill with concern and knew her assumption had been correct. Adam was in love with her best friend.

In her room, Lilith was feeling pretty sure of herself. She'd turned off her heated blanket, which she had used to warm her skin and up her temperature for Sarah.

Pulling a *Ferris Buller's Day Off* on her best friend was not only underhanded but pure genius. After all, how else was she going to get her stubborn friend back on the island with Ben?

Sure, she was going to have to spend the next two days locked in her room, but she had some reading she wanted to catch up on anyway.

When there was a light knock on her door, she tossed her book down and hit the switch on her heated blanket, conveniently hidden under her sheets, and called out that whoever it was could come in.

When she saw Adam, she groaned out loud. "Not you!" She sat up and adjusted her hair.

"How are you feeling?" he asked, setting the covered tray down on her lap.

"Fine. You can leave now." She realized what she looked like, what she'd done to make herself look pathetic for her friend's sake.

Instead of listening to her, Adam sat on her bed and frowned. Then to her horror, he stood up again and started pulling her blankets away.

"What on…" When he uncovered her electric blanket running on full power, he laughed. "So, this is a ruse."

She rolled her eyes and leaned back, crossing her arms over her chest. "Go away."

"But why?" He sat back down next to her.

"I needed a few days off."

"Pourquoi?"

"Oh, stop that thick accent. We both know you've lived in the states for almost ten years now."

He chuckled as he reached over and took the tray from her nightstand and set it on her lap. "Eat." He removed the lid.

Instead of the foul-smelling broth, there was a rich smelling, perfectly baked chicken quarter with mint sprouts and a twist of lime, which sat in a bed of rice and vegetables.

"You knew!" she hissed.

"Oui." He smiled and leaned back.

"How?"

"You looked fine this morning."

She waited, giving him a look of "I don't believe it."

"It was obvious, especially when Sarah came rushing

into the kitchen after talking with Ben. Her face was all pink and I could see her heart racing from across the room. When she told me you were sick… I knew." He shrugged.

"And you didn't tell her?" It was possibly the first nice thing Adam had done for her since arriving at East Haven.

"Who am I to step in the way of love?" His eyes met hers and for a moment, she really did feel light-headed.

CHAPTER 13

He sat on the blanket, watching the star's blink at him and thinking about Sarah. He didn't know his next move, only that he wanted to be with her. His mind wandered over what was waiting for him in Boston.

His townhouse? His parents? His job? He could easily see himself leaving it all without a blink. Everything except Bella. He'd been left alone with his parents and knew just what kind of damage they could cause a teenager.

He didn't dare leave her alone to their devices. Especially since she'd just turned sixteen. His little sister had been growing into her teen attitude for a while, but in the past few months since her birthday, things had taken a sharp turn.

Their parents were growing more distant from her like they had with him when he'd come home from school the summer of his sixteenth birthday with a mohawk and an earring.

Thank goodness Bella didn't have either... at the moment. She had died the ends of her dark hair a deep purple, which had caused her parents to call him in a rage. They had demanded that he talk her down from her ledge and convince her to go immediately to his mother's hair-stylist and have it "fixed."

None of which he did. Instead, he'd asked his sister for a photo and told her how awesome it looked and how much fun she would have with the wild color.

His parents had been livid. But it had been rewarding since his sister had opened up to him even more about some girlfriend issues she was having at school.

"You look deep in thought." Sarah's voice came from just behind him. He turned slightly and smiled at the darkness. He watched her walk into the moonlight and noticed the bottle and small basket in her hands.

"Is that dessert?" he asked, shifting slightly so she could sit next to him.

"Maybe." Her eyes twinkled in the starlight as she pulled the cork out of the wine and poured them each a glass. "Adam could only spare these." She pulled out a plastic container and opened it. Two fluffy pieces of apple strudel sat nestled inside.

"I was hoping to get my hands on one of those," Ben said, taking her glass and moving it aside so she could dish up the rich dessert.

"It's best served with a dash of ice cream, but..." She smiled over at him. "I'm sure we can make do without it tonight." She handed him a plate and then settled back with her own, holding up her fork for him to tap with his. "Here's to hiring a French chef."

He chuckled as he dipped his fork into the pastry. He

waited and watched as she tasted the dessert. When her eyes closed on a moan, he felt his body race with desire.

"Aren't you going to taste it?" she asked.

He set his plate back in the basket, put hers next to his, and brought her lips to his. His tongue brushed across her lips until she opened for him. He tasted the richness, the sweetness, and the desire all at once.

"Mmm," he said against her lips. "More." He dipped his tongue in for another taste.

"Ben," she moaned as his mouth traveled down her neck slowly. She tasted too good to stop. His lips and hands traveled over her, lifting, pulling clothes aside as her hands raced over him, pulling his shirt off.

His fingers shook as he gently pulled her cream slacks down her legs, followed closely by the silk panties underneath. When she lay out in front of him, the moonlight shining down on her skin, he lost his breath.

"Ben," she whispered, reaching her arms up to pull him towards her. He felt her bare skin next to his, and he knew he'd never experienced anything like this before. This much want. This much need.

"I brought…" She reached for the basket. "Protection."

He smiled and held her still. "I've got us covered too." He pulled the small package from his back pocket. Her eyes traveled down his chest just before her fingers followed the same trail.

"I wasn't going to do this, you know."

"Why not?"

"Because I don't like mixing business with pleasure."

"What made you change your mind?" He held his breath as he waited for her answer.

"You," she purred, clearing the rest of his doubts from his brain.

She wrapped her legs around his hips and pulled him towards her.

He knew the moves, knew how to make a woman enjoy him. But here, now, every other instance rushed from his memory. This was different, almost like this was the first time.

He wanted this time, with her, to be something better. Something more.

Pulling back slightly, he ran his hands slowly over her skin. Her eyes closed as his fingertips trailed a pathway over her.

Her fingers moved to the blanket and gripped the soft fabric as he continued his slow torture. Her legs loosened around him, so he moved down, using his mouth and fingertips to please her.

When he covered her with his mouth, her fingers dug into his shoulders.

"Yes, that's it. That's what I wanted." He lapped at her. "You taste better than any wine or pastry," he drawled as she moaned. Her hips jerked with his every move until he felt her body pulse under his fingertips.

Sarah lay on the blanket, under the stars, completely naked and didn't care. Ben had destroyed her. She could still hear her pulse pounding in her ears. Her eyes were too unfocused to see any stars or even the full moon for that matter. Instead, all she knew was the beating of her heart, the tingling all over her body from pleasure, and the way her lungs labored for breath.

Slowly things came back to her. The warm air brushing lightly over her exposed skin. The soft sand and blanket underneath her. The sound of the waves lightly crashing a few feet from them. Ben's fingertips brushing up her sides, over her heated skin. She felt her body quiver once more with desire and marveled at the way he could control her with just a fingertip.

She twisted slightly until she could see him. He was laying on his side, his dark eyes roaming over her body. There was a slight smile on his lips, making him look like he'd enjoyed their venture as much as she had. She knew she wouldn't stop this time.

Pushing on his wide chest with her palms, she shoved at him until he lay flat on his back on the blanket.

"My turn." She smiled down at him.

"Sarah," he warned.

"No, you don't get any say in this." She covered his lips with a fingertip. "Just sit back and enjoy." She drew her finger slowly over his lips, down, over his strong chin. He'd shaved since she'd ran into him earlier. Now, his face was smooth as silk. Her finger traveled down his neck, past his Adam's apple, over his impressive chest. She felt his muscles jump when her mouth replaced her fingers. Her tongue traveled over his slick skin as her hands moved down his narrow waist.

She tugged lightly at his jeans, pulling them down until he was exposed to her. When her fingers wrapped around him, she felt his hips jerk under her light touch.

"I've wanted this," she whispered next to his skin.

"Wanted you." She wrapped her fingers tighter around him, causing a groan to escape his lips.

"Sarah," he begged.

"Now you know how I felt." She moved down until her mouth hovered above him. "You know how much you pleased me and tortured me." She ran her lips over him. His fingers dipped into her hair as his shoulders bound off the blanket.

She took him fully into her mouth, and he growled and pushed her underneath him. He ripped the small foil package open with his teeth and shielded himself. He was inside her before she could catch her breath.

She didn't hear his moan since her own had drowned every other sound out. Her legs wrapped around his narrow hips, holding him, demanding he move as his mouth covered hers.

"More," he begged. Demanded. "I'll have more." His hips jerked with hers as they found a fast pace. She'd never felt her body so much—every breath, every nerve, every ounce of her desire.

When she felt herself building, he slowed, and his kisses became softer, deeper. "I want this to last," he confessed next to her ear.

"Please, Ben," she demanded. She'd been right there. Ready. She needed so much. Her heels dug into his thighs, demanding he move faster.

Her fingers dug into his hair, pulling him back towards her lips. When her tongue dipped into his mouth, she felt him kick up the speed once more and almost laughed out loud with joy.

"Yes," she implored. "More." She repeated his words from moments ago.

Throwing her head back, she felt the moment he let himself go and allowed herself to follow him.

When she finally surfaced again, she realized a few things. One, she was starving. Two, she was cold.

"I hope there's more in that basket than strudel. I'm starved," he said, moving slightly so that the full effects of the breeze hit her. She started shivering.

"Damn," she heard him mumble. "Hang on, let me…" He dumped his sweatshirt over her head and helped her pull on her jeans. "I should have…"

"Don't." She stopped him by taking his hands. "It was perfect." Her teeth chattered slightly.

"Let's head in." He pulled on his own jeans, ready to get up.

"No, I'm much warmer now. Let's stay and enjoy what I brought." She reached for the basket and handed him his strudel and wine. "Adam packed a few other items— grapes, crackers, and some cheese." She pulled out the box of crackers and the container of cheese. "The French sure know how to throw a picnic." She smiled and set the food in front of them. "Am I right?"

He laughed as he plopped a green grape into his mouth. "These aren't as sweet as you."

She felt herself blush slightly, so she stayed busy setting everything out. By the time they had settled back down, her stomach was growling out loud.

"Sounds like you skipped dinner," he joked.

"Yeah, I didn't mean to. The wedding ate up all of my time."

"How did it go?" He leaned back as he enjoyed the cheese and crackers.

"Oh, it was lovely." She sighed, remembering how lovely

the bride looked in her ivory lace gown with its décolletage-framing shoulder straps. Much like the one Sarah had always envisioned she'd wear one day. "The couple did magic tricks instead of wowing everyone with a coordinated dance." She giggled. "And the groom was the bride's assistant instead of the other way around. It was all very funny."

"Guess I missed the show." He picked up the plate with his strudel and finally took a bite. "Wow, this is good."

She picked up her own plate and took another spoonful. "Yeah, but I think the dessert we made was better." She winked at him and he chuckled.

They ate everything in the basket and then wrapped the blanket around themselves to finish off the bottle of wine.

"So, what happens next?" Sarah asked, feeling very sleepy. "You go back to Boston…"

She felt his chest rise and fall. "I turn in my reports, make a few decisions…" He fell silent.

"And?" She held her breath, knowing that he'd already talked about coming back at the end of the month, but unsure of what that really meant. Too many questions flooded her mind. She wanted to shut them out, but something nagged at her to know more.

"I'm not sure. My sister is pretty important to me. I can't imagine just leaving her in Boston with my parents."

She felt her heart kick and rested her hand over the spot to settle it. "I wish I'd had a brother like you."

He was silent for a moment. "From the sounds of it, Rowan filled the spot pretty well."

"Yes," she smiled. "You're absolutely right. I guess I don't show him enough how much I appreciated him being the voice of sanity in the crazy jungle that was my house growing up."

"Your mother doesn't seem too bad to me."

"That's because she has settled down some. She used to rent out the rooms on the second floor."

"And?" He waited.

"To anyone and everyone who wanted. Some paid with cash, others paid with other things…"

"She doesn't strike me as the kind of mother who would put her daughter at risk."

"No, at least she had that." Sarah sat up and hugged her knees. "The rooms were always empty when I stayed there. If she was having some of her guests over, I would be shuffled off to my aunt and uncle across the way. Rowan and I would sneak over there sometimes and peek in the windows, just to see the parties she was throwing. Some of them were pretty crazy. Kind of like teenagers when their parents are out of town."

"Have you ever thrown one?"

Sarah laughed. "I throw parties almost every weekend."

"Any of those for you?"

She shook her head and hugged her legs tighter. "I'm not really into parties. How about you?" She turned her head to look at him.

"Once, in college. It got so out of hand, they called a paddy wagon and hauled half the campus away." He laughed.

"What happened to you?"

"I escaped into a girl's dorm and hid under the blankets with her." He smiled. "Those were some fun times."

She couldn't stop laughing with him as he told her the story from start to finish.

"So, will you bring Bella here, with you?" When he tilted his head, she knew he'd never thought it as a possibility. "There are some really good schools here, even a private school where one of our best presidents sent his children. It's about half an hour away from here, near Freeport."

"I don't think my parents would go for something like that."

"Why not? Didn't you say they sent you off to school? This way, if you're here, she could at least have you close by."

"My future isn't determined yet." He brushed a hand down her hair and she felt torn. Part of her wanted him to take her dream job so that she could have him in her life. But part of her jumped at the idea that becoming manager of East Haven could still be a possibility.

CHAPTER 14

When Ben walked into the dining room the next morning, Sarah was serving a small group of women. He'd wanted to take her back to his room and spend the rest of the night with her, but instead, he'd walked her back to her door and kissed her goodnight.

He could tell she'd needed time to think about things, about what had happened between them. Hell, he needed time to think about it himself. Which he had. Most of the night. After a pretty much sleepless night, he'd watched the sunrise on the cliff side of the island as he ran down the pathway alone.

Now, he was hungry for a meal and here she was, looking damn sexy in a tight pair of black leggings and a long flowing cream-colored blouse.

Had he stopped to really appreciate how long those sexy legs were last night? Why hadn't he?

"Are you going to sit down or do you want your breakfast standing in the doorway?" Sarah joked.

"Sorry," he mumbled. He'd been so preoccupied with

his thoughts, he hadn't even realized she'd walked across the room and stood in front of him. He followed her to a table nearest the fireplace. There was a low flame going, letting off minimal heat. He'd showered and then spent an hour answering emails and making calls before coming down for some food.

"Let me know what you want," Sarah said, setting a menu in front of him.

His hand snaked out and took hers, holding her by his side. "I think I made it clear last night what I want." He saw her lips curve upward in a smile and her eyes soften.

"Yes, you did."

"Can I see you again tonight?" His fingers played over the inside of her wrist.

"I…" She looked around like she was thinking about her schedule. "There's a new party coming in later. They have the main hall booked for another wedding."

"Two weddings in a weekend?"

She chuckled softly. "You should be here during the season. Sometimes we have four or five." She tugged lightly, so he dropped her hand. "I get off early, though, since Lilith has made a miraculous recovery. I'll be done around five."

"Want to meet at the beach again?"

"No." Her smile grew. "Let's meet at the pool near the tennis courts. I have a feeling that, after today, I'm going to need the bubbles in the hot tub." She rolled her neck as she walked away.

He sat there, blankly staring at the menu, trying to get the image of how sexy she was going to look wearing a swimsuit out of his mind and wondering what he could possibly fill up the rest of his day with to kill the time.

As it happened, he was spared sitting around being bored. Shortly after he returned to his room after a rather large breakfast, he received a call from Larry at the office, who needed his help dealing with an emergency. There had been bad weather overnight in South Carolina and the entire first floor of the condo complex Elite oversaw had been flooded.

He spent the next four hours making arrangements for professional cleaning crews, painters, drywall repairmen, and electricians to clean up the mess.

By the time everything had been arranged, he was exhausted and decided a few hours catching up on sleep wouldn't hurt.

An hour later, he was jolted awake when his cell phone rang. Glancing over, he groaned when he saw his mother's number on the screen. Knowing how conversations with her usually went, he sat up and rubbed his hands over his face before answering.

"Hello, Mother." He blinked a few times until his eyes adjusted to the light.

"Are you ill again?" she asked, sounding like the thought annoyed her rather than concerned her.

"No, just catching up on some sleep. I was up pretty late."

"I thought this was a business trip?" Again, with the annoying tone.

"It is. That doesn't mean I can't take some personal time while I'm here."

"As long as it doesn't interfere with your job."

He couldn't stop his eyes from rolling. "Surely you've called me for another reason other than to scold me about managing my time."

"Of course, I have. The Walters are having a party at the end of the month and I've RSVP'd already for you. I know their daughter, Kayla, is coming back from a year in Paris and thought you should make an appearance."

"Mother," he warned. It was an old argument between him and his parents. Kayla Walters was the kind of woman his parents envisioned for him. The fact that he had zero interest in the woman didn't even phase them. Not that Kayla wasn't attractive. She was, simply put, one of the most exotic creatures he'd ever laid eyes on. However, his taste had never really run to the exotic. Besides, everyone except her parents and his knew Kayla had a thing for bad boys. Ben had never really fit into that category either.

Early in high school, they had found out that their parents were trying to push them together and quickly became friends, nothing more.

"Surely you can set some time aside from your very busy schedule..."—more sarcasm— "for a little party."

He tried to think of an excuse to get out of spending an evening in a monkey suit, standing around having boring conversations with stuck-up people who were full of themselves.

"I'll be there," he practically growled out.

"Good, now that that is settled..."—his mother didn't skip a beat— "we've decided to send Bella to Switzerland next term. There's this perfect private—"

"No!" He did growl this time. Jumping to his feet, he almost kicked the nightstand with anger. "You are not sending that kid halfway across the world by herself to go to some stuck-up—"

"Well, a school abroad was perfectly good for you."

His mother's tone never changed. It was like she had been expecting him to blow up.

"You know perfectly well it wasn't. You are not sending Bella away." Sarah's words played over in his mind. "There are some very exclusive schools up here."

"Where? Silver Cove?" His mother's laughter was soft and controlled. "Really, Benjamin. Bella is not going to some backwater…"

"Why not? This school was good enough for a president's kid. Why not Bella?"

"Well…" For the first time in his life, he felt like he was getting through to his mother.

"Think about it. I can visit the campus while I'm up here and collect more information. Besides, having her somewhat close could save you on airfare and tuition."

"If you want, gather some information. We can discuss it with your father when you return home. We'll see you at the Walters' party."

After he hung up, he punched his fist into the air and almost danced around like he'd won the battle. Then he glanced down at his clock and calculated that he had enough time to drive into town and visit the school that day.

Taking a quick shower, he pulled on a fresh suit and made a few phone calls. The first was to the school itself to see if they were open and if he could get an appointment to be shown around the campus that afternoon. The second call was to Jerry to have him pick him up and take him to the mainland.

By the time he walked down to his car, he was actually excited about the possibility that Bella would be so close.

"Leaving us already?" Jerry asked when he followed the man up the stairs after parking his car on the ferry.

"Just for a while. I heard about the private school in Freeport and wanted to check it out for my sister."

"Brighton School is one of the best around. It's been rumored that several presidents have sent their kids there. Not to mention movie stars and some pretty cool rock legends."

"I'm hoping my parents will be convinced to send Bella there, instead of Switzerland."

Jerry made a show of shivering, then whistling. "How old is she?"

"Sixteen." He frowned down at the dark water as they ferry chugged across the open space. Jerry glanced over at him.

"Wow, sending a kid off like that, halfway across the world alone." He shook his head.

"Exactly!" Ben leaned up slightly. "Those were the worst years of my life, being away from my friends and family. I felt abandoned." He sighed and leaned back against the railing.

"It must have been hard on you."

"That's the reason I want Bella to go someplace close. I don't want her to go through what I had to."

"You're alright. You know, when I first met you, I thought… Here comes another city guy with his mind on his wallet. A man who's willing to do whatever it takes for his own personal gain."

Ben laughed. "I guess first impressions aren't always the best."

"But now." Jerry shook his head. "You're alright." The

ferry docked smoothly. "Just give me a buzz when you're ready to head back."

"Will do." He started down the stairs. "Where do you live, anyway? I mean, you come and go at any moment."

Jerry smiled. "I've got my own private island just there." He pointed to a small chunk of green trees. "Whistle Island. It's been in my family for generations."

"And you don't mind being called on at odd hours?"

"Are you kidding? I live for it. Gives me a break from my writing."

"You're a writer?"

"Science fiction. You might have heard of me. I write under JT Whistler."

Ben took a step back and would have fallen down the stairs if Jerry hadn't reached out to steady him. "You're JT Whistler?"

Jerry's smile grew. "You've heard of me?"

Ben could only nod. "I… It's a pleasure to meet you." He held out his hand and shook the man's hand firmly. "I can honestly say, I've read and enjoyed every book you've ever written. What the heck are you doing running a ferry?"

"It helps break up my mundane days and, besides, I enjoy meeting new people like you." Jerry laughed.

Sarah was almost too busy during the day to think about last night. Almost. The fact that Ben kept popping into her head was pleasing and disturbing at the same time. After he'd told her that his future was uncertain, she'd needed some time to think things through. So, when he'd walked her back, she'd made some excuse about an early morning and retreated into her room alone.

Instead of a restful night, she'd lain awake for most of it thinking about what her next step should be. Something kept calling her back to him, something she couldn't explain.

In her mind, she knew it wasn't a good idea to get involved, but her mind wasn't always in charge. Especially when his hands and mouth were on her skin.

She held in a groan and looked around. She was setting up for another wedding party out on the back veranda. Heather and two of the other event ladies they used during busy season were helping. Luckily, they were clear across the area, so her groan had gone unnoticed.

Glancing at her watch, she realized there was less than ten minutes before the guests would be heading down for the party.

"Ten-minute warning," she called out as she stepped up her speed. She enjoyed this part of her job. The calm before the storm, as she liked to describe it.

By the time the first guest arrived, everything was in place. It looked beautiful with the pale blue ribbons and flowers that the bride and groom had requested. They would use the flowers later that evening for the after party, which meant hauling them down on the flatbed cart to the pool area and once more taking time to arrange them.

"Sarah, do you have a moment?" She looked over to see Rodney wiping his hands on an old white handkerchief as he stood in the shadow of a large pine tree.

"Sure, Rodney. Let me just tell Heather I'll be stepping away." The older man stepped back into the shade so no one arriving at the party would see him.

When she found him again, he was standing near the edge of the garden, watching the waves crash below on the beach.

"What's going on? Are you okay?" Concern flooded her mind. Not that she hadn't had plenty of chats with the older man over the years, but he'd never purposely sought her out like this before.

"Yes, I'm fine. Still having some arthritis issues, but once it warms up…" He'd been rubbing his left elbow but stopped. "It's about my grandson, Nathanial. He's gotten himself into some trouble in the city."

"What kind of trouble?" Sarah pulled on Rodney's arm lightly until he followed her to a nearby bench.

"Well," he started again after they'd sat down. "Nothing major, but enough that my daughter is concerned. She's a single mother and works two jobs just to keep food on the table. Anyway, Laura and I got to talking about maybe bringing the kid up here, you know, get him away from the city and all."

"That's a wonderful idea." She patted Rodney's hand.

"I was thinking since it's spring and I usually hire a few other guys to help…"

"Rodney," Sarah interrupted, "if you want to hire your grandson for the season, you don't have to ask my permission. I put you in charge of hiring your own men and I'm going to stick by it."

The smile on Rodney's face was its own reward.

"Thank you." He stood up and she followed since he'd taken hold of her hands. "This will be the opportunity the boy needs to turn his life around. You just wait and see. Besides, who knows, maybe someday he'll be working here full time. After I'm gone that is."

Sarah's laugh was quick. "Rodney, you're not going anywhere. You're too stubborn to die."

The old man laughed and reached over to hug her. "You're a lot like your mother, you know that. I remember the day she first came to East Haven to work. Pretty young thing. Still is. So kindhearted and caring."

"Thank you." Sarah reached up on her toes and placed a soft kiss on the paper-thin skin of his cheek. "Now, I'd better get back to the party. It sounds like things are in full swing."

Rodney dipped his head quickly. "I'll make the arrangements. Nate will start first thing next week."

"I look forward to meeting him." She dropped his hand and started back towards the party, wondering how Ben would have handled the situation if he were manager. By the time the party was over, she had herself convinced that he would have handled Rodney in the same way. After all, his kind heart had been one of the reason's she'd started falling for him. Which was another reason she was full of concern and anxiety? She was, indeed, falling for him.

Hard and fast. That's what her mother had always said about how she'd fallen in love with her father.

"When it's right, it doesn't have to take long."

She'd always assumed her mother was just being… well, herself. But now she was beginning to understand. That fact that she was actually starting to understand her mother made her even more scared and anxious.

CHAPTER 15

When Ben got back into his room a few hours later, he figured since it was nice and warm out, he would switch into his swimming trunks and head down to the pool. He knew it was too early to run into Sarah there, but since he was full of newfound energy, he decided to get a few laps in before his date with Sarah later.

His excitement was due to the successful meeting with the head of the school. Not only had the trip into Freeport been an education, he'd found that the small town held more possibilities than he'd imagined. He'd picked up a local paper and some housing brochures to scan through on the trip back into the city in a few days.

Now, he was not only convinced that Brighton School was the best place for his sister, he was even more convinced that he could see a future for himself nearby.

All he had to do now was finish convincing himself that this is where he belonged and prove to his parents that Bella was better off in Maine than in Europe.

When he arrived at the pool, he was the only occupant. Grabbing a large blue towel off a rack full of guest towels, he set it, along with his shirt and shoes, next to a lounge chair and jumped in the deep end.

The shock of the cool water hitting him only made him feel more alive and determined to crank out as many laps as he could. He'd joined the swim team in his early high school years. But after finding out that Crissy Higgins wasn't going to be on the team, he decided running track was more his style.

Still, as he kicked off from the wall, he felt his blood heat within the first few laps and his mind clear from the task of breathing and keeping his body to the internal rhythm of each stroke. He didn't count the laps or even glance down at his watch to check his time. He wasn't here for competition or even his health. What he needed was a chance to clear his mind from all the distractions, so he could think about the doubts that had begun to plague him —doubts about his life in Boston, his career, and even his family.

Maybe it was sort of an early-life crisis or maybe it was just that he'd become bored. Whatever the reason, he was thinking of making a major life change and one thing the Rothschild's didn't do was jump into anything without weighing the pros and cons.

By the time he felt his body screaming at him to stop, he'd cleared up several things. Resting along the side of the pool, he watched the clouds pass him by as he laid out his plans.

When he saw the sky change to a light pink, his mind changed gears to Sarah and when she would be joining him at the pool. Just then there was a loud splash and water droplets rained over his warm face.

"You looked like you were in dreamland," Sarah said after surfacing. "Been here long?" He watched her move towards him slowly.

"Long enough." His arms wrapped around her body and he felt himself grow with excitement when his hands landed on bare skin. Glancing down, he noticed the light pink bikini and wished he'd seen her outside of the water. Still, he kicked off from the bottom, pulling her towards the deeper water as his fingers continued to play over her exposed skin. "Mmm, you feel so good." He dipped his head and took her lips softly.

"This feels good," she said against his mouth. "The sun, the water, you." She hummed as her hands ran over his back, her nails lightly digging into him, causing his desire to spike.

"If you keep that up," he growled out as her legs wrapped around him, "I can't be held responsible for what someone might see if they happen upon us here."

Her sexy giggle caused bumps to rise over his skin, so he pushed away from her to give himself a minute. She ducked her head under and pushed off to the side of the pool.

He easily kicked his legs and stopped next to her.

"What did you do today?" she asked, a little winded as she leaned against the side of the pool. "I noticed on the way over here that your car had moved."

"I went into Freeport and met with the dean at Brighton."

"And?" She turned towards him.

"I think it's perfect for Bella." He turned around,

resting his shoulders against the side of the pool. "Now if I can only convince my parents…"

She remained silent for a moment. "Does that mean you've made a decision?"

He glanced over at her, not wanting to get his own hopes up and frowned slightly when he heard a group of people heading their way. "I'm still debating. How about we hit the jets?" He nodded towards the hot tub. "I think I outdid myself on the laps and could use the heat on my muscles."

She followed him to an oversized hot tub that sat closer to the ocean. The thick shrubs surrounding the area made it feel more secluded and drowned out the noise from the group splashing in the pool.

"How was your day?" He settled beside her, pulling her closer to him.

"It had its ups and downs." She turned slightly towards him. "Do you know; I believe Lilith faked her illness?"

He tried to hold in the chuckle that rumbled in his chest, but since she was so close to him, she heard it.

"You knew?" She leaned away and frowned up at him. "You were in on it?"

"No!" He laughed. "But I had my own suspicions. When I returned to the island, alone"—he frowned and pulled her closer— "she was determined to get you back here, so we could… work things out." He omitted any further details. "Besides, I would put it past her."

Sarah shocked him by laughing out loud. "You know; Lilith has never done anything like this before. At least not to me." She rested her head back against his shoulder.

"You're not mad?" he asked, brushing his hand down her wet hair.

"No, why would I be?" She let out a soft sigh. "I'm happy the way things turned out."

"Me too." He nudged her until their lips met. When the kiss turned deeper, he thought about the logistics of pulling them out of the hot tub, up the stairs, across the garden, and through the house to his room as quickly as possible. "Not fast enough," he said under his breath.

"Hmm?" she asked against his mouth.

Roaming his lips to her neck, he paused. "It's going to take too damn long to get you upstairs and naked."

She chuckled. "There's always the hidden cottage."

"The what?" He pulled back and looked down at her.

Sarah stood up and tugged on Ben's arm until he followed her. They grabbed their towels and shoes as they passed the main pool area where several of the wedding guests were enjoying the dying sunlight.

She took his hand in hers and pulled on him until he followed her down the pathway towards the beach. Instead of heading left on the path towards the water, she turned right at the large oak and pushed a few branches aside to walk out on a hidden pathway.

"I've been by here several times and haven't seen this pathway before," he said, following her closely.

"That's why only a few of us know about the hidden cottage." She smiled back at him as she continued on the way. When the path turned steeper, he helped her until they reached a small opening in the brush and the cottage came into view.

It was no more than a small wood shack, but a few

years back Tom had allotted the money to have the trim repainted with a fresh coat. The classic wood shingles still looked good and the new windows and door that had been put in a few years back kept the outside looking nice. But it was the inside where all the character was.

"Come on. I have the keys." She pulled her master ring out of her shorts pocket. She led him up the wood steps to the front door.

"It's like something out of a fairy tale," he said when she dropped his hand to unlock the sturdy front door.

When she opened the door, she stood back and let him enter first. "Tom decided to have this redone a few years back. He hid the cost of the remodel in the remodel for the dining room." She smiled. "We've actually rented it out a few times and made our money back."

"You… you rented this out?" He glanced around the small one-room space.

"You'd be surprised. Some couples don't want to spend their wedding night in just any hotel room. Not that ours aren't something to behold, but…" She glanced around and let out a soft sigh. "There is something magical about a small cottage in the woods that no one knows about."

It really was like a fairy tale. The space was small. Tiny to be exact. However, Tom had hired one of the best tiny homebuilders in the northeast. The man had done wonders.

The cabin was narrow and long, which meant that even the smallest of spaces was utilized. By the door was a built-in L-shaped sofa with a wood-burning stove at the end. On the wall to the right was a countertop for a small kitchenette with a built-in booth for dining. The bathroom was in the very back and boasted a nice-sized shower with a long seat.

A wide ladder led up to the top floor, which was nothing more than a king-sized mattress with two large square skylights overhead.

"Wow," Ben said, still looking around. "Who would have known you could make such a small space feel so big?"

Her arms wrapped around him. "Cozy?"

He turned in her arms and she felt her heart kick up a notch.

"If I told you I had a fear of small spaces?"

She laughed and pulled his mouth down towards hers. "You'll get over it," she said, pushing him up against the doorway as her hands roamed over his chest. When he moaned, and his hands started tugging at her bathing suit, she figured he didn't mind the small space.

That was until he started pulling her towards the ladder.

"Um…" He frowned up at the thing.

"The sofa." She tugged him towards the wide pillowed area. When they fell on the soft cushions together, she felt her need for him growing. "Ben," she moaned when he finally freed her from her wet swimsuit. She started to tug on his shorts but had a difficult time with the drawstring.

"Here, let me." He stood up quickly and tossed them off. But instead of coming back down to her, he stood over her. His eyes roamed over her slowly.

"You are so beautiful." She thought she heard his voice crack slightly. Raising her hands towards him, she silently begged for him to come back to her. Instead, he continued to look down at her. "Damn." He frowned down at his shorts. "I didn't bring…"

"My shorts." She smiled and pointed. "Back pocket."

He walked over and took the condoms from her back pocket. "Three of them, huh?" He turned to her and smiled.

"Be prepared." Her smile grew when he returned to her side, running his hands over her skin slowly. He caused small bumps to grow everywhere his fingertips played over her. Her skin grew hot and slick from desire as his mouth trailed where his hands had just played.

"Ben, please." Her nails dug into his shoulders, trying to force him to rush.

"I was wrong," he hummed.

"Hmm?" Her eyes were closed as she paid too much attention to what his fingers were doing to her slick skin.

"I thought I needed this fast, needed you fast. But I'm finding out that slow is a better pace."

"Please." She threw her head from side to side as her fingers dug into the cushions of the sofa. She felt her hips jolt when his mouth covered her when his tongue dipped inside her to lap slowly at her core.

When his finger brushed her tight nub, she jolted, causing his hands to push lightly on her hips, holding her down onto the sofa. "That's it, come for me," he murmured next to her skin. "I want everything. Every moment you want to give. Every second. I want to see your skin warm to my touch, hear your breath hitch when I enter you. Feel you in my arms when I wake up. See you there, looking up at me when I lose myself. I want it all."

Her brain was too foggy to register most of his words,

but when he talked of losing himself, she couldn't hold back the floodgates, as she fell hard and fast.

When her breathing steadied, slowed, he entered her smoothly as his eyes locked with hers. Her breath hitched, and she released it on a soft groan of pleasure.

"I meant it, you know."

She was having a hard time focusing on his face, so her eyelids slid closed.

"Sarah, look at me." He stilled above her. When she did, he brushed a finger down her face gently. "I meant it."

"Yes," she said, not sure if she could stop herself from moving underneath him. Her body screamed out to her to move next to him, glide around him.

When her eyes closed again, she felt his lips press up against hers as he started to move. He whispered into her ear, telling her wonderful things as his hips moved next to hers. When his pace grew, she wrapped her legs around his hips and held on as he took what he needed from her, what she wanted to give him. Everything.

This time when she surfaced, everything was dark. Too dark. The sun must have set sometime shortly after she'd fallen off the edge.

When she made a move, his arms tightened around her. "No, hold still," he grumbled into her hair. Noticing that her hair had dried completely, she wondered just how long she'd been out.

"I need some water," she said, trying once more to wedge herself free.

"I'll get it." It was too dark to see, but suddenly his warmth was gone from her body, causing her to realize that there was still a slight chill in the air.

When the light flicked on overhead, she groaned

slightly and reached down to pick up her shirt as he walked a few steps to get a glass of water for her.

"I could get used to living a small simple life," he said when he turned around. He smiled at her as she pulled on the T-shirt. When it was on, she realized she'd picked up his shirt instead of her own. The shirt hit her mid-thigh and smelled pretty damn sexy, just like him.

"I thought you were afraid of close quarters?"

His chuckle sent waves of heat through her. Then he handed her the glass and she gulped down the cool water, trying to extinguish the heat he'd caused from the inside out.

"It does have its perks."

"Oh?" She swallowed the rest of the water and set the glass down. Ben was still standing in front of her, gloriously naked. Her eyes slowly roamed over him, taking in every beautiful cord, every toned muscle across his chest, his flat stomach. She gazed at his powerful arms and strong legs as he stood with his feet shoulder-width apart. When her eyes traveled back to his face, she noticed the way his hair stood slightly on end from her fingers. He'd had a light shadow of a beard when she'd arrived at the pool, and now it was thicker, darker, making her want to run her fingers over it and enjoy the richness.

"Getting to make love in every room of a house was on my list."

She couldn't stop the laughter, nor the want. Standing up slowly, she walked to him and wrapped her arms around his shoulders. "There's still the bathroom."

CHAPTER 16

The trip back to Boston was a lot better than his trip up to Maine had been. At least he didn't have to deal with a fever and the body aches that had wracked him the first time.

Instead, this time it was his mind that wouldn't stop wreaking havoc. The what-ifs were running through his mind so much that he was finding it hard to concentrate on his work.

He hadn't technically take a week off, but he hadn't stayed on top of things, so he had a lot to catch up on before he hit the office first thing Tuesday morning, including a full report on Sarah Holley. And, since the old man hardly ever came in to the office anymore, he knew he'd probably spend a few hours on the phone to his boss going over it word for word.

He spent the few hours it took to get back to civilization plucking away at his keyboard, trying to summarize what he thought about Sarah and her position at East Haven Resort.

He ended up silently cursing himself several times when he couldn't keep his personal feelings towards her out of the report. He deleted more than a full page when he decided he'd overstepped the personal line.

Finally, only ten minutes before the train was due to arrive at the station, he hit send on the email to his boss and shut down his laptop. When he glanced down at his phone, he was happily surprised to see a text from Sarah. Opening it, he smiled at the picture she included of the hidden cottage.

"Walked over to watch the sunrise. Thought of you. Sarah"

In the picture, with the light from the sunrise hitting the old wood shingle siding, the cottage glowed like it had been sprinkled with fairy dust. The green of the trees and bushes that surrounded the front door seemed almost blinding, as did the bright blue of the sky above.

They had spent their night in the cottage making love multiple times in every room, including laying in the loft under the two large skylights, watching the stars as they fell asleep in each other's arms.

He took a picture of the city out of the window of the train and sent it to her. "Your view is much better than mine. Missing you."

The rest of his time there had been quick. Too quick. Sarah had been busy with work and he'd taken two more trips into Freeport and Silver Cove to look around. He'd even met with a real estate agent. He'd kept that information to himself since he still hadn't made up his mind.

When he felt the train jolt to a stop, he grabbed his bags and headed out. The crispness of the city air hit him first. The smell of petrol, the noise of horns honking, people going about their business. Suddenly, he missed the quiet of the island, the smell of the salt air hitting his face, and Sarah.

As he was letting himself into his apartment, his phone rang. Balancing his bag as he opened his door, he clicked on his phone.

"Hello, Mother."

"It's about time you made it back. You know, I think it's just awful that you were forced to be out of town for so long."

"I didn't mind it." He set his bag down on the countertop in his kitchen and walked over to pull a beer from his fridge. Even though it was just past noon, he knew he'd need the help to deal with whatever his mother had called to talk to him about.

"Is that a beer top? Did you just open a beer at this hour?"

"No," he lied. "It's a sparkling water." He took a deep drink and smiled when she believed him.

"Well, I'd hope not. One week in the country and you're drinking like a sailor. Anyway, I hope you are free tonight for a family dinner."

He held in a groan and rested his head back on the cabinet.

"Why? What's up?"

"We're going to talk to Bella about school in Switzerland."

He shot up from leaning against his counter. "We agreed to talk about the school in Maine before you made a decision." He felt his temper rise.

"That was before your sister decided to start her latest career."

"What career?" He downed a little more of the beer.

"She wants to be a singer on American Idol," his mother said in an exasperated tone.

"Bella does have a great voice," he started but decided a different tactic would be better. "Remember when I was her age? How I wanted to learn how to play the drums."

"Of course. You had your father all up in arms about it. You dragged us to the music store and the second we heard you banging around on those things..." She stopped talking.

The moment he'd tried to play drums; he'd learned quickly that he couldn't keep a rhythm.

"I think if you let her discover something for herself, Bella might just surprise you. Not that she doesn't have a really great singing voice... It's just that we Rothschild's didn't get too much in the way of rhythm."

He thought he heard his mother chuckle, a sound he hadn't experienced for a very long time, but she quickly covered it up with a sigh. "I suppose you're right."

"Still." He decided it was now or never. "I think we should still meet. I wanted to go over a few things."

"Things?"

"How about six o'clock? I'll bring the wine."

"You're always welcome here, you know that."

After hanging up, he took his beer to the shower and tried to wash off the feeling of being stuck on a train for several hours. He crafted a speech to his parents in his mind. However, halfway through his shower, he stopped thinking of his sister's school career and switched gears to Sarah. He wondered what she was doing tonight. If there was a party she was frantically getting organized for. Or if she would spend a few minutes floating in the pool, looking up at the sky and thinking of him.

He took a little longer in the shower than he'd expected, and when he finally got out, he realized he had less than an hour to get dressed, pick up some wine at the store, and make it across town to his parent's place.

He arrived five minutes late, which he knew wouldn't help his cause since his mother was a stickler for punctuality. He rushed up the stairs, hoping the extra seconds he'd save would at least count in his favor.

"Sorry I'm late," he said a little out of breath as he kissed his mother's cheek and handed her the bottle of her favorite cabernet. He shifted the stack of brochures under his arm as he removed his outer jacket and hung it in the closet just inside his parent's front door.

His parents had purchased the large place a few years after he'd moved out of his childhood home, claiming they'd done it because it was closer to his father's work and Bella's school. However, the place was nothing more than a showpiece for his family's wealth. It boasted seven bedrooms, six baths, two parlors, and was in a zip code that was known for its prestige.

"We were about to start without you." His mother turned just as Bella came rushing down the stairs.

"You're back." His sister rushed over to him and gave him a big hug. He could see worry in her eyes but knew that with his mother standing beside them, his sister wouldn't open up to him.

"Yup, I just got back a couple hours ago." He wrapped his arm around her as they followed their mother back towards the large dining room. His mind quickly compared this house to Sarah's childhood home. Even with Sarah's bottom floor being more of a display piece, it felt more like a home than this one did. Here there was no old family furniture or vintage pictures hanging on the walls.

No, his parents had hired one of the best and most expensive decorators to come in and furnish the space. Most of the furniture didn't even look like it had been used in the three years they had lived here. He knew that half of the rooms had sat empty as well.

"There you are." His father looked up from his phone. He was already seated at the end of the table that could easily seat ten people. When his mother took her spot at the other end, he rolled his eyes at his sister, who held in a giggle. Then Bella took his hand and tugged until he sat next to her, closer to their father.

"Tell us all about Maine," Bella started as their first course was served by one of the three people employed by his parents. His mother had never wasted time with cooking or baking. Instead, in the course of his life, they had gone through more than a dozen cooks.

He started talking about his trip, leaving out the slight detail of falling flat on his face in front of Sarah. He did, however, go into detail about the town, the resort, the beauty of the place, and the quaintness of the small towns. He told them about his and Sarah's hike and then, just as the empty plates from the main course were being cleared, he brought up Brighton School.

Bella had glanced down at the brochures many times during the meal, but both of them knew that their parents wouldn't allow them to look through them until the meal had run its course.

"Sounds like you're thinking of going back there?" his father added in.

Ben took a cleansing breath and nodded briskly. "I've been debating it."

"What?" his mother broke in, pushing aside the piece of apple pie that had been delivered in front of her. "You aren't thinking of moving there?"

He felt his sister's hand reach under the table and settle in his. The small comfort seemed to give him the extra strength that he needed.

"Yes, actually I have. I've burned out here, in Boston. I'm the highest I can get at Elite and"—he shook his head lightly— "I'm nothing more than a glorified secretary. Honestly, I'm baffled why I've stuck around so long." He turned back to his father. "It's not that I don't appreciate the time there or everything I've learned…" He felt his sister squeeze his hand lightly. "I think"—he smiled down at Bella, who smiled back— "it's time I went out on my own. Found my own way."

"What would you do? From the sound of it, there's not much in way of jobs up there. Actually, from what you've said, it sounds pretty empty of anything civilized."

He held in a laugh. "Actually, it's quite the opposite." He dropped his sister's hand. "Just take a look at these brochures for the school I was telling you about, Brighton." He handed two to his mother and the rest of them to his father. He handed his sister the one for her. "I'm thinking of a slight change in my career."

"What?" His mother hadn't even touched the brochures, instead looked down at them like they were a snake on her dining table. "Work at the school?"

This time he did laugh. "Why not?"

"And be what? A teacher?"

"I'm not sure."

"Ridiculous! You have no experience teaching."

"Actually. I have plenty of experience. Not only have I pretty much been running Elite for the past few months, I did major in higher education, even though I chose to start the job at Elite instead of following my own dreams." His eyes moved to his father. "Jacob Evans, the current dean, is months away from retirement. So far they've had only two qualified applicants, but after talking with him, I might be open to the idea of sending him an application"

"Why on earth would you want to live in the country?" his father questioned.

"I'm tired of the city, Dad." He reached over and took another sip of his wine, but even that tasted too bitter. What he wanted was a cold beer and the salt air on his face. And Sarah by his side. "There's nothing more for me here." He looked over at his sister. "Besides, the school is one of the finest in the States. I believe it would be more beneficial for Bella to attend Brighton than to be shipped overseas to a school and a culture she'll have no connection to."

He knew an argument would ensue; he'd been prepared for it. What he hadn't planned on was that it would take the course it did. By the end of the evening, he walked back up the stairs to his apartment feeling defeated. Pulling off his tie and shoes, he fell onto his sofa and took out his cell phone.

-I hope your day went better than mine.

He waited a few moments before Sarah replied.

-Same old same old. What happened?

-Talked to my folks about Bella going to Brighton.

-And?

-It sounds like it's a no-go.

-I'm sorry.

-Me too. I miss holding you.

Sarah felt her insides melt when she read his text message again for the tenth time. They had chatted for a while until he'd told her he had an early meeting in the morning. After they said goodbye, she'd lain awake in her bed, rereading his messages.

How was she supposed to move on with her life when the man kept sneaking into it? She was trying to be realistic. Long-distance relationships rarely worked out and since Ben hadn't confirmed or denied that he was coming back to Silver Cove, she had to assume the worse. Which in her case was either-or. If he did choose to come back, that meant she would be leaving to find her own way. She had even started looking at other resorts, some as far away as California. She needed to stand her ground. She had the talent, the drive to manage her own place. Surely, someone out there somewhere could see that in her.

If Ben decided to stay away and not take the manager job, she knew there was a chance of Elite hiring someone else, which meant pretty much the same thing.

Her head had been so twisted since he'd left that she'd spent most of her day in a daze. She was thankful that Lilith and Heather had picked up the slack. Lilith had even pulled her aside and tried to comfort her, telling her that things had a way of working themselves out.

"Don't do anything rash," Lilith had warned.

"Rash? Like what?"

Lilith's laugh had jolted her. "Like quitting."

"Why would I do that?" she'd asked, silently wondering if her friend had ESP.

"Sarah, how long have we known each other?"

"Too long." She smiled at the private joke between them.

"Right." Lilith nodded her head quickly. "And, since I know you, I know enough to question when you're about to do something crazy."

"Lilith, I'm not going to quit."

Her friend chewed her bottom lip as she looked at her through narrowed eyes.

"Fine!" she finally blurted out. "I promise not to do anything without letting you know in advance."

Still, that hadn't stopped her from questioning her next move.

The next day was her last before she had a few days off. However, the day seemed to drag on instead of fly by like most. By the time she'd helped clean up after the last dinner party, she had a splitting headache and her ears were ringing.

Since it was early enough, she sent Jerry a text to pick her up and take her to the mainland. What she needed now was time away from all the questions running through her mind, and she knew she'd find that at home.

Since her overnight bag was already packed, she headed down to the dock to wait for Jerry. She leaned against the wood railing of the dock and stared out at the dark water. She tried to use her mother's breathing exercises to help clear her mind, but not even meditation was helping her much.

"Hey," someone said behind her, causing her to jump and spin around.

She laughed at herself as she held her hands over her heart. "Oh, I didn't hear you come up." She smiled at Nate, Rodney's grandson. He was taller than any seventeen-year-old she'd ever seen. His blond hair was long, and he'd even tied it back with a strap. He had his grandfather's blue eyes, but that was as far as the resemblance went. Everything else about the kid was different. He dressed in baggy clothes like he was trying to hide the little extra bulk he had. He had a few pimples and the fact that he had a pack of cigarettes in his hand told her he'd paid someone to buy them.

However, even though the kid had just started working that morning, she could tell he had taken an instant liking to the job. Which, in her book, made him okay.

"Sorry, I was just grabbing a smoke." He threw the cigarette butt into the water.

"How was your first day on the job?"

"It's okay. Are you going somewhere?" He nodded to the bag at her feet.

"Yes, home for a few days."

"Oh, I thought…"

She smiled at him. "Several of us have families on the mainland. We work a split schedule."

"Oh, you're married?"

She laughed. "No, my mother lives in Silver Cove. She runs a shop. Serenity's. You should swing by sometime. It's on Main Street."

The kid's eyes lit up. "Sounds cool."

They both turned as Jerry sounded the horn on the ferry.

She reached down to pick up her bag, only to bump solidly into Nate as he reached down to pick it up for her.

"Sorry," she said and stepped back to allow him to take the bag.

"I guess I'll see you around," he said, handing her the bag.

"Sure." She smiled as she walked over to her car and tossed her bag in the back seat.

She waved at Nate as she loaded her car onto the ferry.

"How'd the kid do?" Jerry asked as they pulled away from the dock.

"So far so good," she said as she looked back towards the island. She could just see the red tip of another cigarette burning at the end of the dock.

"Lilith tells me you're thinking of leaving us," Jerry said, glancing over at her.

She held in the string of curses and knew that her friend was going to hear them firsthand next time she saw her.

"No," she finally said, wrapping her arms around herself.

"Oh?" Jerry turned towards her. "This doesn't have anything to do with city boy, does it?"

Closing her eyes, she leaned back against the railing, letting the salt air cool her down.

"Don't get me wrong. I like the guy."

Her eyes flew open. "You do?"

"Sure." He smiled. "The way he was talking about his sister… Anyone who wants to protect someone they love that much is okay in my book."

Sarah remembered how Jerry's younger sister, Lori, had died, and she felt her heart skip. "I'm sorry," she said, reaching over and touching his hand.

"I wasn't there for Lori." She felt his muscles bunch

under her fingers. "Your guy seemed pretty determined to keep his sister close. To protect her against their parents."

She nodded, not knowing what to say. Jerry was one of the few people in town that hadn't blamed Rowan for Lori's death. Maybe it was because Jerry had been Rowan's alibi during the hours his sister had been hacked up. Even Jerry's parents had questioned her cousin's innocence.

"He really loves her." She took a few cleansing breaths. "Which does say a lot." She felt her own feelings for Rowan and knew how she had felt when everyone in town had turned on him, claiming he was a murderer.

"I don't know him as well as you, but if you're thinking of leaving your home, leaving us, because of him"—Jerry dropped a hand off the steering wheel and put it around her waist in a light hug— "don't."

uesday mornings always sucked. Maybe it was because most of the seasonal rentals ran from Tuesday to Tuesday, which meant more paperwork, more phone calls, and the possibility of more problems. Add in the extra meetings he had scheduled and the fact that he'd been out of town for over a week and he knew the day was going to be a disaster.

When he walked into his office, Cheryl, his assistant, jumped immediately. She was a short woman with arms and legs as thick as an elephant's trunk, but she always seemed able to outrun him. She handed him a stack of phone calls that had to be returned immediately.

Since he was still feeling deflated from the dinner at his parent's last night, his outlook for the day was pretty gloomy. That was until he walked into his office and saw his boss sitting behind his desk.

"Morning, Ben," the old man said, getting out of his chair.

"I'm sorry, I should have told you that Mr. Harrison

was here to see you," Cheryl said, starting to back out of the room.

"Yes, next time I'd open with that," he said quietly. He took the stack of phone messages from her and shut the door. "It's good to see you again." He set the papers on his desk and reached out his hand to take the older man's.

He knew that when Carl Harrison was in the building, it didn't matter if it was your office or the bathroom, the man would make himself right at home. After all, he did own the entire building. So, Ben took the chair in front of his own desk and watched as Carl sat back in his office chair.

"I got your report last night." The man leaned back in the chair.

"And?" He waited, leaning slightly forward.

"I can't say that I disagree with you. Everything coming out of East Haven has confirmed your findings."

"So, you're going to give Sarah Holley the job?" He didn't realize he was holding his breath as the old man's eyes roamed over him.

"Maybe." He crossed his arms over his chest. Carl Harrison was anything but meek. The man reeked of power and wealth. It wasn't just the fact that he'd come from around the Rockefeller era, but that the man had made something of himself out of nothing. Class, power, wealth all screamed from every pore, down to how he held himself and the way he carefully chose his words. "I've read this"—he held up a stack of papers, which Ben could only assume was his report on Sarah— "several times now. But what I really want is to hear it all from you. Directly."

Ben had known it was coming. So when he started his

well-prepared speech, he was shocked when Carl interrupted him.

"Yes, yes, that's all well and good. But I don't want a practiced speech." The man shocked him and stood up to walk towards the window. Then he turned and shocked him even further. "Have you had coffee yet?"

"Um, no. Normally I…"

"Good, let's get out of here." He picked up his jacket and pulled it on.

"Sir, I have a lot of catching up…"

Carl interrupted him by opening the door. "Cheryl, Mr. Rothschild and I will be taking a few hours. Have Mr. Parrish fill in for him while we're out."

"Yes, sir," Cheryl said eagerly.

Ben shook his head and followed the old man out of the building.

When they hit the sidewalk, Carl turned and started walking instead of heading to the black car that was waiting for him. "We'll walk," he told the driver, who immediately nodded and shut the door.

"Sir?" Ben kept up with him. "What's this all about?"

The man looked over at him. "How long have you worked for me, Ben?"

Ben thought about it. "Almost three years, sir."

"And in that time, you went from pushing papers to my second-in-command."

He could argue that he wasn't technically directly under him but held his tongue instead.

Carl stopped in front of one of the older diners along the street. "Martha and I used to eat here every morning." He reached over and opened the door for him. He remembered that Carl's wife, Martha, had passed away last year from cancer. Ben walked through the door and looked around. He'd eaten here plenty of times himself. The food was good enough, if not a little greasy.

They sat in the back corner booth and silently looked over the menus.

Once their order was in, Carl looked over at him.

"I'm dying."

"Sir?" Ben was instantly worried.

"Not this minute." The old man chuckled, a deep rich sound. "The doctors say I might last the year out."

"I'm sorry, sir."

Carl shook his head to stop him. "No, it's okay. When you get to be my age you look around and realize everyone you've ever known or loved has gone before you." He sighed and leaned back in the seat. "Besides, everyone has to go sooner or later."

Ben nodded. "What can I do for you?"

"Well, that's why we're sitting in this greasy dinner." Carl smiled as he leaned forward. "I want you to tell me everything you can about Sarah Holley. Down to the most intimate details."

Ben leaned back and frowned at the older man.

"Oh, don't give me that look. I can see it in your eyes." He chuckled. "It's the same look I had when I met my Martha." The smile slipped a little. "Actually, it was one of the reasons I sent you up there instead of Jim Parrish or one of the other guys. They're all married and older. You, on the other hand," The man crossed his arms over his chest. "I've been watching you for a while."

"Sir?"

"I've known your folks for a while."

Ben nodded. "Yes, sir." He knew how long his father

had played kiss-ass to the Harrison family, back when he and Carl's son had been friends.

"I never really cared for your dad. He's too much of…" Ben could tell the older man was searching for the right words.

"A kiss-ass?"

Carl shocked him by letting out a loud burst of laughter, enough to get several heads in the diner turning their way.

"Exactly!" The older man pointed in his direction. "I'm not saying he didn't serve his purpose. Your father kept my son in his place for a while." Carl shook his head and sighed as he frowned. "A man is not supposed to bury his son."

"I'm sorry, sir." He didn't know what to say next.

"Tell me about Sarah."

"I don't understand your interest in one of your employees. I mean, don't get me wrong. The woman is phenomenal at her job. But why the personal interest?"

"You never knew my Johnathan. Did you?"

"No, sir. He died when I was too young to remember."

"Yes, you would have been just a boy. Still, in diapers, I'd imagine. Johnathan was a lot like you. He was so young, so smart, and very determined. When I sent him up to Silver Cover, shortly after we purchased East Haven, I expected him to report back to me within the month if the place was worth keeping or selling."

"What happened?"

"The damn kid fell in love instead." Carl shook his head and held in a chuckle. "Broke his mother's heart when he told us he was going to stay up there and run the place."

Something in Ben's mind clicked and he felt his heart sink.

"Sarah?"

Carl looked at him and bobbed his head. "Of course, back then, Martha was really calling the shots. Still, we thought we saw right through the young woman and we were both sure she was after nothing more than our bank account. So, naturally, we decided to cut him off, giving her no excuse to stick around. Instead, she wound up pregnant and Johnathan ended up with cancer. Shortly after he found out, we traveled up there to talk some sense into him. Force him to come back to Boston where he could be seen by some of the best doctors. But, he wasn't about to leave his new family."

Ben held in his anger. What kind of man would force his son to make such a hard decision?

"I can see by the look you're giving me that you don't agree with our tactics." Carl exhaled and then paused while their food was delivered. Instead of eating, he pushed the plate aside as a sadness washed over him. "I'm not going to sit here and explain my parenting methods. I've made my fair share of mistakes in my life. That was the biggest one to date. Now, however, I'm staring at my own mortality and I have a few choices to make. I can live the remainder of my short life with regrets or I can rectify them. I'm choosing the later."

"What can I do to help?" Ben leaned forward, ignoring his own food in front of him as he listened to the old man's plans.

The three days at home did wonders for her mind and body. She even joined in her mother's yoga classes a few times. Her mother, being the woman, she was, had known immediately that something was up. She'd snuck into her room and placed lavender and lemongrass oils in her lamps and had even gone far enough to place a packet of bergamot leaves under her pillows.

However, much Sarah liked to disagree with her mother's tactics, she had to admit, the soothing scents had helped calm her down. Not to mention they made her feel right at home since it was something her mother had been doing her entire life.

Still, the first few days back at work, the tension started building up again. Several strange things had happened while she was gone. She wanted to believe it wasn't Rodney's grandson that was causing problems, but the kid was the only new person to the island, other than the guests. She doubted anyone who would pay their going nightly rate would stoop to breaking into the employees' storeroom and stealing items.

She'd had a talk with him and tried to gently hint that if the incidents continued, there would be a more thorough investigation, which could possibly lead to the police being called.

Nate assured her that he had nothing to do with the break-in, and part of her wanted to believe him. She didn't want to bring it up with Rodney since she knew how fragile the older man was and how much he was hoping his grandson would turn his life around.

The busy season had officially started, which meant that instead of an entire week off, she was looking at only spending three nights on the mainland. But she didn't mind. Especially since being busy kept her mind off of Ben and the decision she was going to be forced to make soon.

It had been over two weeks since he'd left. Every evening they spent talking on the phone or texting one another.

"I've got this party to go to this weekend. I really wish you could be here to go with me," he said. Just hearing his voice did things to her insides. Things she wanted to deny were happening, but she just couldn't bring herself to lie to herself.

"Party?" she asked.

"Yes, longtime friends of my family. Their daughter has finally come home from a few years overseas."

"Um…"

"I can arrange the whole trip. You wouldn't have to do anything other than pack." He sounded like he was almost begging.

"I don't—"

"I've already asked Lilith and she's assured me she can cover for you."

"You did what?" She sat up a little too quickly, causing some of the water from her bath to spill over the edge of the tub.

"Easy. She called my office for something else and I just happened to mention the party. She's the one that suggested I convince you to go."

Sarah sat back a little and thought once more of how to strangle her meddling best friend.

"Well?" he said after a moment of silence.

"How fancy is the party?"

"The Walters always have tux kind of parties. If you

want, you can come into town early and we can do some shopping."

"Who are you?" It came out as a whisper. His only reply was a chuckle that sent more waves throughout her body.

"Be ready Friday morning."

"Ready?"

"Lilith knows the details. Now, on to something more important…" There was a moment of silence. "It sounds like you're in the bath," he said in a breathless tone.

"Yes." It came out as a whisper.

"Good, then you can skip explaining what you're wearing and instead start describing all the fun parts to me instead."

CHAPTER 18

Friday morning Sarah stood on the helipad with her mouth gaping open as Ben jumped out of the private helicopter.

"What?" She blinked a few times. "How?" She pointed to the sleek black Agusta helicopter.

"Don't ask," he said, taking her bag from her hands. He leaned in and placed his mouth over hers for a quick kiss. "We'd better get going if we plan on having enough time to shop before the party."

"I... I don't understand," she said once they were sitting on the soft tan leather seats. "Whose helicopter is this?"

"A friend's." He smiled, trying not to let any of his well laid-out plans show in his eyes.

She turned to him with a slight frown. "Whose?"

"Does it really matter? He loaned it to me for the duration of our trip. Be thankful you don't have to sit in a crowded train for four hours." He took her hand up to his lips and kissed the soft skin, wishing there was a dark wall between them and the pilots. Even so, he pulled her closer on the seat and wrapped his arms around her. "I've missed you," he said, running his mouth over hers slowly.

"Me too." Her fingers were in his hair, holding him to her. "How long is the flight?"

He couldn't stop the chuckle. "A little over an hour."

"Damn." She sighed.

"I know," he growled next to her skin as the helicopter rose up over the water.

Even though the trip back to Boston was a lot quicker than his trip up there, it still seemed like the helicopter couldn't move fast enough.

When they touched down, he realized that they had better hit the shops on the way back to his place if they planned on buying Sarah a dress for the night.

As she slid into his car, he watched her relax back in the seat and couldn't stop smiling. "Tell me about your week," he asked as they pulled out of the parking garage of the private building they had landed the helicopter on.

She talked as he drove to some of the shops he knew his sister and mother frequented. She told him about Rodney's grandson starting and how someone had broken into the storage area where they housed a lot of supplies for the employees.

"We have an honor system in place there. There are items for employees to buy, like shampoo and tooth-brushes. They take what they need and mark it down on the list, so the amount will be deducted from their check. So far, since I put the system into place, we haven't had any problems. Actually, we've even started supplying items such as candy and cigarettes." She stilled for a moment. "That's how he…"

"What?" Ben frowned as he glanced over at her.

"I didn't think." She closed her eyes and leaned her head back. "I was wondering how Nate was getting cigarettes."

"Don't tell me you have them just sitting out in the employee's store area?"

"No, of course not." She frowned at him. "They are in the locked back room. Only a few employees have keys. We store the cigarettes and liquor back there."

"And?" he asked.

"Well, Rodney would have a key to the room. When someone broke in, they didn't take much from the storeroom. A handful of candy bars, a few bags of chips. I didn't even think to look in the back room," she said as she picked up her phone and punched a number.

"Lilith? Hi… yes, we made it to Boston. Yes, it was a surprise, which I plan on talking to you about later." He watched as her smile grew. "Okay, enough. We've just landed. I will answer all your questions later. For now, I need to you go into the employees' store and take stock in the back room." She was silent for a while. "Yeah, my thoughts too. Okay, thanks." She hung up and tapped her phone against her thigh.

He reached over and took her hand in his, stopping the movement. "There's no use in worrying about it until Lilith lets you know. Until then, how about we do some shopping?" he asked as she pulled into the parking garage at the shopping area.

He watched her relax back. "I don't really like shopping," she said, causing him to laugh.

"Good. Neither do I. But we'll make an exception this time." He pulled her across the seat and placed another kiss on her lips. "Let's try to make this quick since I can't wait to get you back to my place and naked."

He felt her shiver in his arms and knew she was as affected as he was.

"I think I'll buy the first dress I try on," she hummed.

It wasn't the first dress, but it was pretty damn close. They had found a sexy gold and white off-the-shoulder dress, which made her look like a goddess. The second she stepped out of the dressing room with it on, he knew he wanted to buy it for her, along with the sleek gold open-toed shoes she was wearing. The long white skirt floated around her legs every time she took a step, making it look like she was walking on a cloud.

"You look… amazing." He almost gasped it.

"Of course, you'll need to stop next door to purchase the lady some appropriate jewelry," the store clerk said as she straightened the hem of the dress.

"Yes, of course." He winked at Sarah, who only looked at him with a worried glance.

"You don't have to buy me any of this," she said as they walked out of the store, laden down with boxes and bags.

"I don't have to do anything." He took her hand and tugged until she followed him into the jewelry store.

They found a perfect necklace and matching earrings for the dress. "These are perfect for either a formal or casual party," the clerk said.

"This is too much," Sarah said, carefully removing the earrings. "Really, Ben, I can easily…"

"We'll take them." He smiled at the clerk and took Sarah into his arms. "Let me do this small thing for you." He gave her a quick kiss, which turned into a slower one when the clerk stepped away to wrap the items. "Just say thank you so I can take you home."

"Thank you," she said, wrapping her arms around his neck.

Sara felt her nerves grow when he parked his car in his building. The fact that the elevator was the nicest one she'd ever seen told her what to expect from his apartment.

When they stepped out of the elevator, she was shocked to see that there were only two apartments on his floor.

"You have half the floor?" She glanced at the two doors, one on either end of the hallway.

"Yes," he said, shifting the boxes in his hand so he could unlock the door.

"How long have you lived here?"

He set the boxes down and hung the dress on the back of the door. "Almost two years." He set his keys down and took her into his arms. "From my calculations, we have exactly four hours before we need to get ready for the party."

She smiled. "What do you think we could do to eat up some of that time?" she purred against his neck.

"Hmm, I was thinking maybe Monopoly?"

She chuckled, then gasped as he lifted her up easily into his arms and quickly carried her through his impressively large apartment. She only got a glimpse of it as he rushed down a wide hallway towards his bedroom.

He stopped just short of his bed as his mouth descended towards hers. The kiss was soft, slow, and spoke of the passion he would show her in the next four hours.

He delivered everything he promised and more. By the time they stepped into his large glass shower together, every muscle in her body was on the verge of turning to liquid. She'd never been more relaxed in her life. But then he started running his soapy hands over every inch of her wet body, causing every muscle to tense and light on fire for his touch.

"You're going to make us late," she warned, trying to keep the soap from her hair out of her eyes.

"We can stand to be fashionably late," he said against her skin.

"Not since it will take me about an hour to manage my hair and makeup."

He groaned and glanced at the clock and then groaned once more. "Fine but promise me we'll leave the party early." She felt her heart kick and wrapped her arms around him tighter.

It took her just under an hour to twist her long hair up in what she liked to call her modern-day Cinderella hair. The front was pulled back away from her face as the back hung down her back in loose locks. She added the two silver bobby pins to the sides and added the beautiful diamond drops with their matching necklace.

When she slipped on her shoes, she wondered if that was just how the fairytale character felt getting ready to go to the ball.

When she stepped out of his bedroom, fully dressed, she held in a slight gasp of shock.

Ben stood in front of a wall of windows that over-looked the bright city lights of Boston's harbor. You could actually see the lights from the ships and boats below them. But that wasn't the best view. The best view was Ben himself. The man looked damn sexy in a black tux. He could have given any Bond character a run for his money.

"All you need is a sexy British accent and a martini in your hand."

"Not to mention the sexy woman by my side," he said with a fake accent as he walked over and took her into his arms. "Score one," he said after he kissed her passionately.

"Is that your gun in your pocket… or are you just happy to see me?" she purred next to his ear.

"That's it, we're staying in." He took her hand and started back towards the bedroom as she laughed and pulled away.

"Take me to your party so we can flirt with one another across the room and drive each other crazy." She tugged on his hand until he stopped moving.

When he turned back to her, his smile was contagious. "Now you're talking." He held out his arm for her to wrap hers through.

"For the record," he said after they were in his car and on the way through downtown Boston, "I'm going to apologize in advance for tonight."

"You don't have to." She smoothed the skirt of her dress, thinking of what he'd told her about his family. "You've met my mother."

"Yes, but…"

"Ben," she interrupted, "no matter what your family says or does, I've learned one thing over the years. They don't define you."

"Just remember what I said. How I apologized in

advance," he said, steering off the highway, keeping his eyes locked on the road.

"I will, but you didn't have to," she murmured as she wondered what she'd gotten herself into.

"On the plus side, you'll get to meet Bella." He reached over and took her hand in his. Just the simple touch reassured her.

"I'm looking forward to it." She realized she was even more nervous about meeting his sister than she was about meeting his parents. Maybe because she knew that he held Bella so much higher in his heart than he did his folks.

When they pulled into a gated community, her nerves spiked. She'd never seen homes this big before. Which was saying a lot since the home she'd been raised in was the largest in the county.

She bit her bottom lip as he drove slowly through the streets until he pulled into a large circular driveway full of lights and cars.

"Are you ready for this?" He turned to her, taking her hand in his.

"I suppose so." She swallowed slowly as he got out and opened her door for her. He helped her get out and made sure her dress didn't get caught in the door.

"You look amazing," he whispered next to her ear just before he rang the doorbell.

"You too," he added just before the large double doors slid open.

A tall frail-looking woman in a long emerald green dress stood just inside the doorway as the lights flickered off her emerald earrings and jewelry. When she saw Ben, she smiled. "We were beginning to wonder if you'd changed your mind about coming."

"Sarah, this is Debra Walters. Debra, Sarah Holley."

"Oh." The woman's smile fell enough to tell Sarah that she hadn't been expecting Ben to bring a date. "How lovely." She held out a hand and took Sarah's in a very light handshake. "The party is in full swing. Your family is back in the music room talking with Kayla." The woman stood back, letting them into her home.

The entryway alone was the most impressive thing Sarah had seen. It was grander than East Haven and Holley Hall put together. Sarah held her breath as they followed the woman past an impressive three-story staircase, through an even more-impressive study, and into a two-story music room with a gold inlaid ceiling. Large crystal chandeliers hung down, flooding the room with soft light. There was a grand piano sitting in the rear of the room against three very large, very beautiful etched windows. The two-story fireplace was something directly out of a glamorous movie from back in the day. She half-expected Clark Gable to be leaning against the mantel, smoking a cigarette and flirting with half the women in the room.

There was a small group of people in the room. The men were all dressed like Ben, in suits or tuxedos. The women in the room, much to Sarah's relief, were in long flowing dresses very comparable to hers.

Ben reached down and took her hand in his. "Easy," he whispered. "Over there, that's my parents by the fireplace and my sister is the one in the blue dress talking with Kayla, in the pale pink dress."

She inclined her head slightly, hoping her jaw would unlock soon. She held onto Ben's hand a little tighter as she glanced around the room. His parents were talking with an older gentleman who was leaning slightly on a cane. She'd never seen someone who reeked so much of power before. Figuring it was Debra's husband and Kayla's father, she followed Ben around the room as he introduced her to a few people on their way towards the fireplace.

Finally, they stopped in front of his family and Bella and Kayla joined them in front of the fireplace.

"Mother, father, Bella, this is Sarah Holley. Sarah, my parents Juliette and Thomas, and my sister Bella Roth-schild." She shook each of their hands as she felt their eyes roaming over her, no doubt looking for anything they could hold against their son. "This is Kayla Walters." She shook the woman's hand, noticing how soft and small it was compared to her own. Then she turned to the older gentleman. Her hand reached out to take his and, after a moment of silence, Ben said. "Sarah, this is Carl Harrison. Your grandfather."

CHAPTER 19

Sarah heard Ben's parents gasp before his words registered and sunk in. She felt a wave of spikes rush through her entire body before she realized she had forgotten to breathe. Her hand slipped from Ben's as she jerked back a full step.

"Sarah." The older man's eyes watered up as she looked at him, her mouth gaping open.

"I…" She closed her mouth and shook her head. "I…" She rushed from the room, heading towards the main door, only to feel a hand on her arm.

"In here," someone said, tugging on her arm until she was pulled into a large sitting room that was connected to a bathroom. She walked over and splashed some cool water on her face as she took deep breaths, trying to steady her emotions.

"Are you okay?" She felt a hand come to her shoulders and glanced up into the mirror to see Ben's sister Bella rubbing her shoulders.

"I…" She closed her eyes and felt a tear slide down her cheek. "I never expected to see him again."

"Ben told me," Bella said, causing Sarah's eyes to jerk open.

"He told you, but kept it from me?" She turned to his sister and crossed her arms over her chest.

"It wasn't because he didn't want to tell you. It was because your grandfather demanded it."

Sarah felt her heart skip once more. "I don't understand." Just then there was a slight knock on the door.

"Sarah?" Ben called out to her through the door. "Is everything alright?"

"Go away, Ben," Bella called out to him. "We need a moment."

"Bella," he started, but then there were muffled voices and the hallway turned oddly quiet.

"No doubt my mother ushered him off to quiet down all the drama," she said leaning against the countertop. "Are you okay?"

Sarah didn't trust her voice, so she just nodded instead.

"Do you need some water?" Bella looked as if she was going to get up.

"No, I'm fine. Just a little shocked. I didn't mean to cause drama."

"It isn't your fault. It's your grandfather's." Bella crossed her arms over her chest and frowned. "Do you know, now that the word is out, I bet my folks will love you."

She frowned over at the teenager. "Why?"

"You're the heir to the great Harrison fortune."

Sarah shook her head. "No, I'm not. My father was

disowned." Then her temper spiked. "They turned my father out because he fell in love with my mother."

Bella smiled. "There you go. I knew you had a spine."

This time, instead of a gray filter over her eyes, Sarah was seeing red. "That man in there is responsible for all the pain, all the heartache my father went through the last few months of his life." She felt her body begin to vibrate with anger.

"Whoa," Bella took her shoulders. "Think. There has to be a better way then storming into a dinner party and yelling at an old man."

That stopped Sarah cold. "Are you sure you're only sixteen?" She frowned down at the dark-haired beauty, who just laughed at her.

"I have a really awesome brother."

Sarah's eyes narrowed. "Whom I'm pissed at, as well."

"Don't be. It broke his heart not to tell you the moment he found out about it."

She wasn't sure what to say to that, so she closed her eyes and took a couple cleansing breaths like her mother taught her.

"What was that?" Bella asked once she opened her eyes.

"Pranayama breathing. It's a form of breathing associated with yoga. It helps me get rid of the anger, stress, and pain."

"Does it work?"

"We'll find out if I don't kill your brother and my grandfather by the end of the night." She walked over to the door and opened it as Bella laughed behind her.

When they joined the rest of the group back in the music room, she felt oddly back in control of her emotions.

When Ben reached for her hand, she laced her fingers together behind her back instead.

She immediately saw the change in the way his parents looked at her. Instead of judging, their eyes were full of sympathy and concern. His mother even tried to wrap her arm around her shoulders but ended up dropping them when Bella walked over and took her hand to drag her towards the piano.

"Sorry for that," Bella murmured. "Mother wouldn't know how to comfort a kitten. I just knew I had to help you out," Bella said sitting on the piano bench.

"Do you play?" Sarah asked, running her fingers over the keys.

"Yes, you?"

"Some. We had a baby grand in our den for years. Until my mother sold it to make room for her yoga classes."

"What a shame. I'd love one in our house, but…" She sighed and rolled her eyes towards her parents. "They're pretty dead set on not letting me follow my dreams."

"What are your dreams?"

"To sing." The girl's smile grew.

"Why don't you play something. If you feel comfortable?"

"Here?" Bella frowned as she looked around the room.

"Sure. Why not? I mean, we are in the music room."

"I couldn't…" The girl started to say.

"If I could be in the same room as my grandfather," she said softly, "then you can sing in a room of people who know you and are supposed to love you no matter what. Besides, if this is really what you want, your heart would burst if you didn't at least try."

"Burst?" Bella gave her a look like she wasn't buying it.

"Well, maybe not burst." Sarah chuckled and squeezed Bella's arm. "If we find something I know, I can help if you need it."

They took a few minutes to look through the music and found a copy of Elton John's Tiny Dancer.

"I learned this one," Bella said. "I think I can handle it by myself." She took a few deep breaths.

Sarah smiled at her memories of playing the song with her grandmother by her side.

"Good luck," she said as Bella set the music up.

Sarah stood and clapped her hands. "Hello, everyone. Thank you for your attention. At this time, Bella Rothschild would like to sing a song for you." She stood back and nodded for Bella to proceed.

When Bella's fingers began to play over the keys, Sarah's heart stretched out to the girl. She had talent. Then she opened her mouth and began singing and tears formed in Sarah's eyes. The girl's voice was smooth as silk.

Sarah's eyes met Ben's from across the room and she couldn't stop the smile that formed on her lips. He blinked a few times and then started moving across the room towards her. When he stopped behind her, his arms wrapped around her waist as he pulled her close. They swayed to the music and held one another.

Bella continued to play as tears leaked down Sarah's face. When the last note rang out, the silent room erupted with applause.

Bella stood up slowly and reached for Sarah's hand as she took a bow.

✳

"Thank you," Ben said when he finally had a chance to pull Sarah out of the room. He leaned down and brushed a soft kiss over her lips, wanting more than just a stolen moment but knowing it would be some time yet before he could get more.

"For?" she asked.

"Bella. I…" He glanced back towards the room, where his sister was still surrounded by a group of people telling her how wonderful her singing and playing had been. "I didn't know how wonderful she was until tonight. The last time I heard her sing…" He chuckled. "I guess she was about ten." He shook his head. "Let's just say she's come a long way in six years."

Sarah laughed and held onto him. "She's grown up. Hopefully, now she'll have the power to stand up for what she wants."

He thought about the night he'd tried to persuade his parents to let her go to Brighton and frowned. "Maybe. But after tonight I know I'm willing to give another shot at trying to convince my parents."

"Maybe after tonight, you won't have to do much talking."

He sighed and wished that was the case. "How mad are you about tonight?"

She dropped her hands from his shoulders and took a step back. "I was pretty mad."

"And now?" He shoved his hands into his pants, wishing more than anything they could find a place to talk privately.

"Now, I'm going to see what he wants. Bella told me it

was his idea to keep tonight from me. What I want to know is why."

"He..." She stopped him from talking by covering his mouth with a finger.

"It's not for you to tell."

"No, I suppose it's not." He held still as he watched her take a few deep breaths. "You really have to teach me how to do that," he joked once he saw all her anger leave her eyes.

She smiled and reached out for his hand. "If you're lucky, maybe I'll show you later tonight."

When they moved back into the room, Sarah tugged on his hand until they crossed the space and stopped directly in front of her grandfather.

"I'm sorry about earlier. As you can imagine, it was quite a shock to see you again."

Carl inclined his head slightly as the people he was talking to disappeared. When Ben tried to move away, Sarah held onto his hand.

"Now, I'd like to know exactly why you've brought me here and why you didn't want Ben to tell me you'd be here."

Ben watched a slight smile form on the older man's lips. "You're a lot like your grandmother, you know."

"No, I don't. I only met the woman once." Sarah's chin rose slightly.

"It's a shame we couldn't work things out." Ben noticed the hurt and pain come into Carl's eyes and knew the second Sarah saw it too.

"Yes, it is."

"We were so hurt after Johnathan passed. He was too young." Carl took out a white handkerchief from his pocket and wiped his eyes. "My Martha was a stubborn woman. She passed early last year."

Ben watched Sarah swallow as she nodded. "I'm sorry to hear that."

Carl looked up as he tucked the handkerchief back in his pocket. "We need to do some talking. Not here and not tonight."

Sarah's chin rose once more. "Where and when?"

Just then a bell sounded from the next room, and Mrs. Watson announced that dinner was ready.

"I'll be in touch. Until then, let's see if we can enjoy dinner with people we hardly know." He held out his arm for Sarah to take. She hesitated for a moment, but then she wrapped her arm in his and walked with him to the dining room.

"Better be careful," his sister said coming up next to him and taking his arm. "Looks like the old man is going to steal your date."

"I think I'll allow it for a while." He smiled down at Bella. "You impressed me tonight."

He watched the smile grow on her face. "Yeah?"

"Yeah, now I'm even more determined to get you into Brighton than before. Did you have a chance to read through their music brochure I brought you?"

"Yes." She almost squealed it. Then she cleared her throat and nodded. "Yes, I did. It's quite impressive," she said in a softer tone, causing him to smile.

"Think we can gang up on the folks to get them to change their minds?"

"Hit them from both sides?" When he nodded, her smile returned. "Take no prisoners," she whispered before disappearing to the other side of the dinner table, leaving him to sit between Sarah and his father.

It was nice listening to Sarah and Carl talk most of the way through the meal. Carl was leaving out major details, such as the fact that he owned Elite Resorts International and that Sarah and Ben actually worked for the old man. But he'd agreed to go along with Carl's plan, which meant keeping more secrets from Sarah until the time was right.

He'd been nervous about tonight on so many levels. He had even questioned keeping her away from the party altogether. But his promise to Carl had forced him to follow through. That and his sister's constant begging to bring Sarah so she could meet her.

If that teenager knew that he had such a soft spot for her, he was pretty sure the power would go to her head. He glanced across the room towards Sarah and thought the same thing about her. There wasn't anything he wouldn't do for the two of them.

That knowledge shocked and scared him, causing him to almost spill his drink. The party had retired after the meal into a large sitting room. Sarah had been pulled over to sit between Bella and Kayla as they chatted about Kayla's travels and her time spent in Paris.

Ben was sitting near his father, Carl, Martin Walter, Kayla's dad, and two other gentlemen.

"I hear you're thinking of closing Elite?" Martin said to Carl.

"What?" Ben had been so shocked he hadn't realized he'd said it out loud until Carl coughed loudly to cover the sound.

"You know what they say about rumors, Martin."

"That's good to hear. I was actually hoping you'd have

a position for Kayla." He glanced over at his daughter. "Now that she's back, she'll be looking for work soon."

"That or a husband," his father chimed in, causing Ben to glare over at the man.

"Don't start that up again, Dad."

"No." His father shook his head and then glanced over at Sarah. Ben watched as a gleam entered his father's eyes. "Looks like you've already got yourself a good one there."

Ben's eyes narrowed as he watched his father. He could just imagine the wheels turning in his father's head as he plotted how to get his son to marry the grand-daughter of the man he most admired. One of the wealthiest men he'd ever known.

CHAPTER 20

By the time Ben pulled his car into his parking garage, Sarah's mind was dull. Too much had happened over the last few hours to even replay in her own head.

"I think that somewhere, someone is rewinding and editing the tape from tonight. Then they're adding the cheesy soap opera music and laugh reels."

Ben chuckled and helped her out of the car, then pulled her close. His arms felt so wonderful around her that she didn't mind that they were standing in a dark parking lot.

"I think most of it would end up on the cutting floor."

Her smile grew as she twisted a lock of his hair around her finger. "Why, Ben Rothschild, you devil you," she said in her best southern accent. "You knew all along that my estranged grandfather, whom I hate, was going to be at the dinner party tonight." She stopped and dropped her hand and the laughter. "This is where I would slap you." She dropped the accent and frowned down at her hands. "But I just can't muster the anger."

His free hand took hers as he used a finger to raise her chin until they were eye to eye. "I'd deserve it."

She dipped her chin in acknowledgment. "Yes, you would. But I can't hold it against you. Not when I'm happy it happened."

He took her hand and started walking towards the elevators. "You are an amazing woman, Sarah."

She laughed. "I'm not so sure about that."

He pulled her into the elevator, straight into his arms. "Trust me. You are."

She reached up and wrapped her arms around his head, pulling him down for a kiss. "Thank you."

"For?" He leaned back to look into her eyes.

"For tonight."

"You're welcome." He moved down again to take her mouth. She felt her body respond to his and heat flooded her veins.

"Ben?" she said against his mouth.

"Hmm."

"I think this is the part of the show where the couple tears each other's clothes off."

He chuckled against the soft spot on her neck, just under her ear, causing her desire to spike.

"Far be it from me to get in the way of a good scene." Just then the doors slid open. Ben took her hand and walked a little more quickly towards his door.

Once they were safely inside his apartment, she attacked. Her arms wrapped around his shoulders as he pushed gently until her back was up against the door. His hands roamed over her shoulders, then tugged slightly on the zipper to release the dress to pool at her feet.

"My god," he murmured as he took a slight step back

to glance at her. Since the dress had called for it, she'd only slipped on a sliver of white silk below.

Just the way his eyes roamed over her caused her skin to heat. When his fingers came up to run gently over her, her eyes closed and she leaned her head back against the door.

"Ben," she whimpered when he dipped his finger below the patch of silk covering her. Then she was gasping his name as he dipped them into her heat. His mouth covered hers in a hungry kiss that took her breath away.

Her nails dug into his jacket as he moved her to the brink so quickly. She didn't have time to think or to gather herself before he was pushing her over the edge. Right there, inside his front door, and he was still fully dressed in his tuxedo.

When her head rested on his shoulder and she was gulping for air, she moved to push off his jacket. He stood back and quickly dispensed of it and then slowly took off his shirt. His eyes were locked with hers the entire time. She found the impromptu striptease more erotic than anything she'd ever experienced before.

Her shoulders were still up against the door. To be honest, if she wasn't leaning back on it, she would have slid to the floor in a pool like her dress.

Ben toed off his dress shoes, kicking them to the side as he reached for his belt and slowly removed it. Her eyes zeroed in on his hands as he slowly lowered the zipper of his pants.

When he nudged the pants down his legs, her eyes roamed over every part of him. He was wearing those black boxer briefs she loved on him. Then he tossed his pants away and reached for his shorts, causing her to hold her breath.

When he stood in front of her, as naked as she was, she finally took air into her lungs.

Moving slowly towards him, she reached out a fingertip and ran it over his pecs. His muscles jumped under the feather-light touch. Walking slowly around him, she ran her hands and fingers over every inch of him.

"Sarah." She heard the warning in his tone but continued her exploration, which was just as exciting to her as his striptease.

"My turn. I want to enjoy you." She ran a hand over his tight butt and moaned when he flinched under her fingers. "Mmm, gotta love a guy that can do that to his ass." She smiled as she walked back around to wrap her arms around his shoulders.

He surprised her by picking her up and carrying her to the sofa.

"The bedroom's too far." He fell with her to the over-sized leather cushions and then his mouth covered hers.

She wrapped her legs around his hips, holding him, guiding him to where she wanted him, where he belonged.

"My god," he repeated when he plunged into her quickly. She threw her head back on the onslaught of emotions that attacked her when he joined with her. Her mind screamed to be cautious, but her body was in control at the moment, telling her to let go of it all, to give him everything she had.

"Sarah don't hold back," he commanded next to her ear.

"No," she huffed out. "Never." She felt herself on the edge and wanted him to follow her. Reaching up, she sank her teeth into his shoulder, then ran her tongue over the same spot and felt him convulse above her just as she let herself fall.

Ben was trying desperately to think. But since he was still fully embedded in Sarah's softness, his brain wasn't cooperating. That, and the fact that he didn't want to move couldn't move yet, was causing him some stress.

How could a woman he'd only known a short time destroy him so thoroughly? How had it come to this so quickly? Love?

Did he even believe in such a thing? Why not? After all, his parents claimed to love one another. Even though they had never really shown that much affection for their children, they had always backed one another up and stood by each other's side. But Ben had never believed that was all there was to love.

He mustered up the strength and pulled himself up far enough to look down at Sarah. Her blonde hair had fallen from its clips and was pooling around bare shoulders. He brushed a blonde strand away from her face and leaned down to place a kiss on her closed eyelids.

"It's amazing how much power you have over me," he said when her blue eyes opened and focused on him.

"Hmm." She moaned. "I think that door swings both ways." Her fingers ran over his back, holding him to her.

"I've never had someone like you." He shook his head. No, that's not what he meant. "I've never felt this way about someone before."

He felt her stiffen as her hands stilled on him.

"Ben?" she started. He could see the fear behind her eyes and knew she wasn't ready for his heart. Not yet anyway.

Leaning down, he placed a soft kiss on her lips until he felt her relax again. "Soon," he promised against her skin. "You'll understand, but not until you're ready. Until then, just know that I'm there already." He leaned up and looked deep into her eyes. He kissed her again and then gathered her up and carried her into the bedroom, so he could spend all night pleasing her more slowly.

When he woke, the bed next to him was empty. He heard his shower running and smiled. As he joined her under the warm spray, he couldn't stop himself from thinking about a plan to get her to feel the same way he did.

For the first time since he'd left Silver Cove, he'd slept wonderfully. Either it was because Sarah had been wrapped around him or because he'd finally made up his mind.

"What happens now?" she asked as they sat at his breakfast table, eating the scrambled eggs and toast he'd made while she'd dried her hair and dressed.

"Well, unfortunately, the helicopter is scheduled to leave in about two hours since you're needed back at the resort." He frowned, trying to hold in the rest of this thoughts.

"No, I mean, with my grandfather?" Upon his blank look, she set her fork down and pushed away her almost empty plate. "He said that you would let me know what happens next."

"Right." He needed a moment, so he picked up their plates and took them to the kitchen.

"Ben?" She wrapped her arms around him, stopping him from washing them.

"Hmm?" He closed his eyes and held onto the feeling of her holding him.

"What's wrong?" She nudged him until he turned around.

"Nothing," he lied. "Carl, your grandfather, wants you to return to Silver Cove. He told me he'd be in touch with you in a few weeks."

She slowly nodded, her arms still wrapped around him. "And?"

He shrugged. "I'm not sure what comes next. He hasn't shared that information with me yet."

She smiled slightly. "Okay, what about you?"

"Me?" he questioned.

"Are you coming back to Silver Cove?"

"Yes." He watched as emotions flooded her eyes. Her hands dropped from him as she took a step back.

"Then you've decided…"

"Yes, I have a few things to wrap up here, first. But my plans are…"

Just then his phone rang, and he cursed the interruption. Walking over, he answered when he noticed his sister's number.

"Hey, Bella. What's up?"

"Ben, thank god. You have to come help me. They're actually packing me up!" Bella cried.

"What?" Worry shot through him. "What do you mean?"

"Mom and Dad. They are upstairs packing my stuff. Ben, they bought me plane tickets for tonight."

"To?" He felt his anger grow.

"Where do you think?" His sister's voice grew lower. "You have to stop them. They said I embarrassed them last night and it was the final straw."

He glanced over at Sarah and thought about things. "I'll be right there."

"Hurry, Ben." His sister's voice cracked and he knew it was serious from the tone of her voice.

"What's wrong?" Sarah asked, walking over to him and resting her hand on his arm.

"My parents are going crazy. They're packing Bella up and shipping her to Switzerland tonight."

"That's horrible. I thought that after last night…"

"Bella said that it was because of last night," he broke in, as he rushed back into the bedroom to change and pull on a jacket. "I'm sorry to cut your trip short. I can drop you off at the helipad, so I can head over there to straighten this out."

"I understand." Sarah quickly gathered her stuff, tossing everything except her dress in her overnight bag. She hung the dress back in the bag and zipped it up and then tossed it over her arm and followed him out of the building.

"I didn't mean to cause trouble," she said once they were in his car on the way to the Elite building.

He glanced over at her with a frown. "You had nothing to do with this."

"I'm the one that got your sister to sing last night," she said as she looked down at her hands in her lap.

"Sarah." He reached over and took her hand in his as he stopped at a light. "My parents were just looking for an excuse to ship Bella off. Remember what they did to me? I think they don't like having responsibilities stare at them.

Don't worry, I'll figure something out. No matter what, Bella is not leaving the country today."

He grabbed the wheel and tightened his hands as he prayed that he could come up with the right words, the right argument that would make his parents see it his way.

"I hope so. For what it's worth, I really like Bella."

He parked his car in the garage at Elite and turned to her. "Thanks. I could tell that she really liked you too."

She smiled and took his hand.

"I'm sorry I won't be flying back with you."

"It's okay, I understand." She leaned over and kissed him.

"I'm sorry we didn't have more time together too."

She nodded, holding her lips next to his. "Me too."

"I'll walk you up."

"No, I know the way. Go, deal with your family."

He smiled and then held her face in his hands and pulled her back for another kiss, this time taking it deeper. He showed her everything he felt for her, everything he wanted for them in their future. Hoping she understood, he pulled back and watched her get out of the car and head towards the elevators. She turned and as the doors slid closed behind her, she waved and blew a kiss.

CHAPTER 21

*S*arah took a deep breath since Ben had just knocked the breath from her lungs with that kiss. Leaning back against the elevator wall, she closed her eyes and tried to gather her thoughts.

When she realized the elevator hadn't started moving, she opened her eyes and pushed the top floor button. Her fingers paused over the etched lettering. *Elite Resorts International* was in silver lettering above the entire elevator console.

Elite? This building belonged to Elite? She glanced around the elevator and wondered why she hadn't seen it yesterday when they had arrived. Then she remembered how into Ben she'd been. How she'd been so distracted by just seeing him, being with him that she hadn't really even looked around.

Hitting the button for the lobby, she decided since she had time, she would make a detour and walk through and see the building of the place she and Ben worked for. After all, she'd never been to corporate before.

When the doors opened on the main floor, she let out a quiet whistle. Since it was Saturday, she would have thought that the building would be empty. Instead, there were people everywhere. A young woman with jet-black hair sat behind a glass countertop answering phones and looking very official.

Sarah thought about turning around and hitting the top button to the building but instead stepped out to get a better look.

Walking over to the computer screen board, with numbers and names on it, she searched for Ben's name and smiled when she found it.

Benjamin Rothschild, General Manager.

Then her smile fell away when she noticed the name directly above Ben's.

Carl Harrison, Chairman/CEO

She felt, actually felt all the blood drain from her face. Her hands shook as she held her bag closer to her chest.

Her grandfather? Her grandfather owned Elite Resorts International? So many questions popped into her mind. When her head began to spin, she closed her eyes and leaned a hand on the wall to steady herself.

"Are you okay, miss?" someone asked.

She straightened up and took several cleansings breaths. "Yes, thank you," she answered without looking at the person. Gathering her bags, she marched out of the building.

Her mind, no longer foggy with questions, was only filled with anger. How had she worked for a company her entire career and hadn't known her grandfather was the CEO?

What was even worse, Ben knew. That thought stopped

her cold, causing the people behind her to almost bump into her back. Looking back, she noticed the outside of the building for the first time. It wasn't one of the tallest buildings downtown, nor the prettiest, but it was there, rising to the sky with all the others. It had shiny windows that sparkled in the sunlight and on top of it all, in clean blue letters it said Elite International.

She looked up and noticed that the helicopter was landing. The one she was supposed to ride in back to Silver Cove. Hurt and anger mixed inside of her.

Her heart sank as she realized just how Cinderella had felt when her silver coach had turned back into a pumpkin.

Raising her chin, she turned around and marched towards the train station, even more, determined now than ever to take back her life and make the choices for herself.

When she settled in the seat next to a young couple with a crying baby, she ran her mind over the tasks in front of her.

First things first. Tomorrow morning Elite International would get Sarah Holley's resignation. When the train started to move, she rested her head back as the noise around her dulled and faded.

When her phone rang, she ignored it and turned the volume off. She didn't even glance out the windows as she sped back to the place where she'd grown up, worked, lived. All of it had been a lie. Everything.

She'd believed for her entire life that she'd made her own path. But she'd just been a puppet. What was worse to think about was the fact that Ben had actually taken the job as manager. That her grandfather had trusted him rather than his own flesh and blood.

Had her grandfather's hatred for his son's decision to

fall for Crystal been that bad? He hadn't seemed like it mattered to him anymore when she'd met him. Maybe it had all been a show?

She felt anger and hurt kick up a notch. He had arranged to meet her there, at a dinner party, rather than meet her in private. Maybe it was his way of controlling her once more. After all, what civilized person would yell at an old man in a room full of strangers?

Then her mind turned towards Ben. She'd been denying it for a while, but now the truth was staring back at her. She was in love. Plain and simple. There was no more hiding her feelings especially since her heart was currently breaking.

He'd fallen into her life and she'd never imagined she could ever feel the way she did about someone like him so quickly. Their short time apart had been a test. When she'd seen him again in Boston, she'd known. Just known. She'd held off telling him, afraid of how he would respond. Knowing that it had all moved too fast.

That didn't stop her heart from hurting now that she knew she was going to have an empty spot where she had silently dreamed he would be. She knew what she had to do, but still, something nagged at her to try another way. To hold out in hopes that something magical would happen.

Her mind wandered to her mother and how she had chosen to live, floating like a butterfly on the wind, never choosing her own path in life and love. Sarah had done everything in her life to avoid turning into someone like that and knew she had no other choice than to break all ties with the town and people she loved.

By the time the train jerked to a stop, she questioned

once more if she could follow through with her plans. Glancing around the station, she realized that even here, she felt at home. Like she belonged. She'd ignored that feeling most of her life, always telling herself that she was the outsider. That people were silently laughing behind her and her mother's back. But, in truth, it had only ever been a handful of kids that had done so.

Her mother's shop was successful enough that the doors had stayed open for well over fifteen years. Along with her yoga classes, her mother made enough to survive and continue living in one of the biggest homes in Silver Cove.

The cold air hit her face, making her realize that she'd forgotten her jacket at Ben's apartment. Another loss hit her. Since she'd left her car at East Haven, she pulled out her credit card and rented one, knowing the price would hit her hard if she was going to follow through with leaving Silver Cove.

Instead of driving to the docks, she pulled the rental up in front of Holley Hall. The place was lit up with lights, reminding her that it was Saturday night and her mother would have one of her many yoga classes over. Resting her head against the steering wheel, she let everything out finally.

All the hurt, anger, and disappointment pooled from her eyes as she cried.

She jolted when there was a light knock on the window.

"Serenity is that you?" Rowan stood outside her car, frowning down at her. When he noticed her tears, he jerked open the door and pulled her into his arms.

"What happened?" His arms tightened around her.

"Did something happen in the city? What did that man do to you?"

"Yes, no." She pulled back and wiped her nose on her sleeve. "It wasn't Ben."

He rubbed his hands up and down her arms. "You're freezing. Come on inside." He pulled her towards the house directly across from the bigger one.

When they stepped inside, the warmth and the smell of a fire burning hit her.

Rowan walked over and dumped a throw blanket on her shoulders. "Go sit by the fire while I make us something to drink."

She nodded as she moved blindly towards the heat like a moth. Sitting down on the ottoman in front of the flames, she watched the wood burn and listened to the fire crackle. Her face and her fingers warmed quickly.

"Here," Rowan said, handing her an oversized colorful mug. "I've added a shot of whiskey." He smiled as he sat next to her and wrapped his arm around her shoulders. "So, tell me what happened."

She took a sip of the tea and moaned as the whiskey finished warming her body up. Then she leaned on his shoulder and cried once more as she told him everything.

"What do you mean she never showed up?" Ben barked into the phone.

"I'm sorry, sir. I've checked with the main floor receptionist. No one matching her description was seen coming or going for the building. The pilot assured me that he was at the helipad on time. He waited for over an hour for her."

After hanging up, he tried Sarah's cell once more. He'd been calling it since he'd first found out that she'd missed the ride back to Maine. Worry was beginning to eat at him.

"Did you find her yet?" Bella asked. Worry dominated his sister's eyes. She was no longer concerned for her own future but only focused on what could have happened to Sarah.

"No. I should have waited for the helicopter or at least walked her up to the pad." He felt like hitting or kicking something.

"Ben, you couldn't have known," his mother said from across the room as she and his father waited impatiently to finish their family discussion.

Without a word to them, he turned to Bella. "Go pack your things."

Bella's eyes heated for a split second, and then she caught up to his line of thought and quickly disappeared.

"Finally," his father said behind his back. Ben turned on him.

"I don't think you fully understand what is going on. I'm taking Bella with me. She's not going to be shipped off like I was. She'll decide herself what school she wants, what career she wants." He crossed his arms over his chest and listened patiently to his parents start to argue. When Bella came rushing back down the stairs with two large bags flung over her shoulders, he walked over and took one from her.

"Argue all you want, but she's coming to stay with me until you two can decide you want to be parents instead of letting someone else raise your children." He opened the door and ignored his parent's threats as he and his sister walked out.

"What's the plan?" his sister asked when they were both settled in his car.

"First, we're stopping by Elite to see if we can find Sarah."

"What if she's not there?"

He glanced over and frowned as fear caused his heart to jump. "I don't know."

"Maybe she went home a different way?"

He tossed Bella his phone. "Call East Haven. See if she's checked in yet."

Bella searched through his contacts until she found the right one.

"Hello, this is Bella Rothschild calling for Sarah Holley."

His sister's eyes met his briefly. "I see. When do you expect her back?" More silence. "Yes, thank you. Please have her call my brother Ben immediately when she returns. Thank you."

Bella turned to him and frowned. "She's not there."

Just then his phone buzzed, and Bella fumbled with it to answer.

"Hello," Bella answered. "Yes, wonderful! Thank you." She dug in her purse for a pencil and paper. "I'm ready." He glanced over and saw her write down several numbers. "Thank you, Lilith."

His heart fluttered in his chest. Images of possibilities flooded his mind. He didn't know what he would do if anything happened to Sarah. Loss was something he didn't think he could handle. Especially since he hadn't had the opportunity to tell her how he felt.

"Lilith?" he asked, hope springing up hard and fast.

"She gave me a few numbers to try."

He listened as she called the first two with no luck. Sarah wasn't back in Silver Cove. The third number was to her cousin Rowan.

"He says he's going to check and see if her car's back across the street. Then he'll give us a call in a few."

Ben pulled into the Elite parking garage and yanked on his parking brake just as Joe, one of the security guards, walked over to his car. He rolled down his window to talk to him.

"Thought you might be stopping by. I talked with a few people in the building and Marquita, the HR Director, remembers seeing a woman that fits your girl's description shortly after you would have dropped her off."

"Where?" He started to get out of the car.

"In the lobby. Marquita said the woman looked very pale like she was about to pass out."

More worry flooded him. "Where was she? Did Marquita see where she went?"

"She says after she was done looking at the directory, she marched out of the building like it was on fire."

He felt his heart do a somersault. "The building directory?" he asked, already knowing the answer.

"Yeah, we've got that new one in the lobby. You know, on the big flat screen."

He closed his eyes and remembered it well. He'd been so proud when his name had appeared directly under her grandfather's.

"Damn," he muttered.

Just then his phone rang, and instead of letting Bella answer it, he grabbed for it.

"Hello." He felt his heart race.

"Oh, hey, Ben. It's Rowan."

"Hi, Rowan. Did you find her? Was her car there?"

"Um, yes and no. Looks like she rented a car. She was sitting in it out front, crying. I've got her over here in front of the fireplace warming up. She's like an icicle."

"Can you keep her there?" he asked.

"Um, sure. Her mother has yoga tonight, so I doubt she'd want to go over there with a houseful of strangers."

"Thanks, I'll…" He glanced over at his sister, who quickly nodded. "We'll be there as soon as we can. Thanks, Rowan, for being there."

"No problem. But if I find out this has anything to do with you, you might regret the trip up here."

"Fair enough." He hung up and filled in Joe and helped his sister unload her bags. He pulled out his cell phone one more time and decided he had to make one more call before heading up north to make things right with Sarah.

His mind playing over and over exactly what he wanted to say to her. What he'd been keeping from her. What he wanted and exactly how he felt.

By the end of the day, Sarah would know exactly what she meant to him and what he would do to keep her in his life.

CHAPTER 22

After spilling the entire story to her cousin, she felt completely drained. When Rowan suggested she move to the sofa and lay down while he cooked them some dinner, she didn't hesitate.

Her eyes were burning and even her throat felt scratchy. He'd covered her up with one of their grandmother's quilts. It smelled so much like home that she'd fallen quickly to sleep as she waited.

She jolted awake when the doorbell rang.

"I'll get it," Rowan said, getting up from the chair across from her. He had a book and a cup of coffee sitting next to him. She realized he must have been watching over her while she slept and felt guilty for ruining his Saturday night.

Sitting up, she pushed her hair out of her face. When she heard who was at the front door, she stiffened. Glancing over, she frowned at her grandfather, Ben, and Bella walked in the front door.

"What are you doing here?" she asked, keeping her eyes on her grandfather.

"I invited him," Ben said, stepping over and sitting in front of her on the ottoman. When he reached for her hands, she jerked back.

"When, exactly, were you two going to tell me everything?" she scoffed.

"Why don't we head into the kitchen and see about some hot chocolate?" Rowan asked Bella, who quickly followed him out of the room.

Her grandfather walked over and stood next to Ben. "I wasn't going to tell you until everything was settled."

She tilted her head in question. "Settled?"

Ben leaned closer to her. "You scared me," he interrupted.

Her eyes moved to his face. "I… I didn't mean to," she said after she noticed the worry behind his eyes.

"You didn't get on the helicopter. You weren't answering your phone. We called the resort, they had expected you back hours ago. No one knew where you were. If you were safe."

Sarah closed her eyes and thought about all the phone calls she'd missed on the trip home. All the responsibilities she'd ignored.

"I needed some time." She sighed.

This time when he reached for her hand, she let him take both of them in his. He brought them up to his lips and brushed his mouth across her knuckles. "Sarah, let us in for just a moment."

Her eyes flew open. "I can't afford to." Her gaze flew between the pair of them. "I trusted you." She nodded to Ben. "You kept secrets from me."

"On my strict orders," her grandfather jumped in.

"And you." She turned to the older man. "You own Elite?" When he nodded, she asked her next question. "You never sold East Haven?"

"No. After your father died, we transferred the title of the resort into the holding company."

"Holding?"

He walked over and took the seat that Rowan had abandoned. After settling back, he continued. "The day we met with your father at East Haven all those years ago, we agreed to move the resort out of his name into the holding company, Elite International."

She shook her head. "I don't understand."

"Did your mother never tell you?" he asked.

"My mother knew?" More hurt and anger bubbled deep down. She'd never really talked about her grandparents with her mother. Actually, she'd purposely avoided talking about that day so long ago. She'd been too afraid to find out all the details. Instead, she'd just assumed she'd known what had happened.

"Elite International would hold onto East Haven until your twenty-fifth birthday, which, if my memory serves me, is in a month." She dipped her head in agreement. "After which, if we deemed you fit, everything would be transferred into your name."

"Every…thing?" Sarah felt her head spin. "The resort is mine?"

"More than just the resort." Ben moved over and took the seat next to her. "Elite International. Your grandfather…"

Her grandfather coughed, interrupting Ben. "Sorry." Ben glanced towards the older man. "I'll just go…" He nodded back to the kitchen where they could hear Rowan and Bella laughing. Ben kissed her quickly on the lips before she could decide if she was going to allow it. "We'll finish our conversation later."

"Now," her grandfather said after they were left alone in the room. "You know the logistics pretty much. However, you're still missing some facts. Fact one. I loved your father as much as I loved your grandmother. Both of them were hardheaded as a bull."

"Something tells me you could easily fall into that category as well," she interrupted.

"You'd be right." The man jerked his chin quickly. "But I'm also man enough to admit when I've screwed things up. And I've screwed this up." He waved his hand between them. "Screwed it up from the moment I saw you twenty years ago. You were sitting on the front porch steps in your Sunday dress." He paused to smile at the memory. "The one with the yellow flowers on it." His eyes dulled, and she knew he was reliving the moment. "Fell hard and fast for you the moment I saw the blonde curls and the toothless grin."

She chuckled, causing him to lose the memory. "Well." He cleared his throat again. Of course, your grandmother, Martha, was having none of it. She was too angry that your father had run off and ruined all of her plans to marry him off to the Rothschild's daughter."

"Ben's family?"

"His aunt. It's a damn good thing that didn't happen. His aunt turned out to be…" He stopped talking and glanced towards the kitchen with a whisper. "Well, let's just say, she isn't particularly the mothering type."

"None of his family appears to be," she added.

"That fella in there is going to be the exception. And if he has anything to do with it, he's going to make sure that young girl in there follows his footsteps."

Sarah smiled. "I'd agree with you on that." She felt her heart melt a little more. Isn't that why she'd fallen so hard and fast for him?

"So, anyway, Martha was determined to drag our son into the better life by marrying him off to a very prestigious family, but Johnathan had other plans. He came up here to see if he wanted to take over running the resort, and in the process met and fell in love with your mother. Martha tried to convince him to return home until you came along. We even threatened to cut him off from the family money, but at that point, he'd already turned a mighty profit and was easily making his own way. Apparently, your mother's family had quite the influence and didn't hesitate to help out as well."

"They've been a part of Silver Cove for many generations."

"Yes, well." He cleared his throat again.

"Would you like some tea?" she asked, concerned.

"No, I'm fine." He waved her off and continued. "The day Johnathan called to tell us about the cancer was one of the worst days I can remember." He pulled out his white handkerchief and wiped his nose. "Martha was sure that if he'd agree to come back into the city, we would be able to find the right doctor or the right medicines."

"There was nothing we could have done," Sarah recalled.

"No, of course not. But Martha couldn't handle losing him any more than I could. We came up here on his prompting to meet with him about your future. Yours and East Haven's."

"You yelled at him," Sarah accused.

"Yes, I sure did. He wanted to hand over everything to you right then and there. What does a child know about running a large corporation or a resort?"

"Nothing." Sarah's voice sounded hollow.

"Exactly!" The older man pointed and then rested his hand back on his knee. "After you barged in and yelled at us, Johnathan finally came to his senses and agreed to put the businesses in a trust until you were old enough, with the agreement that when you reached a certain age, you would start working on the island. He had an old friend agree to talk you into it, just in case you strayed."

"Rodney?" She felt her heart skip. "He's the one that told me about the job opening. He's the reason I…" Her hand moved up to her head to steady the spinning.

"So, now that the time was approaching, I sent Ben up here to check up on you. To make sure you're ready for the transfer."

She tilted her head sideways. "There's something else you're not telling me."

He chortled and inclined his head. "Looks like all those years of smoking a pipe have finally caught up with me."

"Cancer?" she asked.

When he dipped his head in agreement, she felt her heart sink. She felt robbed. Here was her grandfather, the man she'd grown up hating. The man who, in her mind, had taken everything away from her. She'd just found out that he'd only been protecting her, and she was going to lose him before she really had a chance to know him.

"How long?" she asked.

"I've got some time yet. But I wanted to get this whole business finalized before I go," he answered.

"What happens now?" she wondered.

"Now you let us do what we came to do," Ben said from the doorway.

Sarah's eyes moved to his. They were red and still slightly puffy from crying. He could see a distant sad look behind the blueness.

"Which is?" she asked, shifting slightly on the sofa.

He walked over and sat next to her, taking her hand in his. "We've still got some legal issues to deal with." He glanced over at Carl. "Some papers to sign. But if all goes well, everything will be transferred back to your name by your birthday."

The room was silent for a moment. Sarah glanced over at her grandfather. Ben looked over at the old man and could see what she did. He looked tired. His face was slightly paler than when he'd arrived at the helipad over an hour ago. He was constantly clearing his throat and looked like he could use a good night's rest.

"I'd like you to stay, if you would, for at least the night," she added.

"I'd like that," Carl answered.

"I was kind of hoping that we could all stay. I'm not a hundred percent sure, but my folks might have put a warrant out for my arrest, seeing as I just kidnapped my sister," Ben added.

"You didn't kidnap me, you rescued me," Bella said from the doorway.

"I don't think they're going to look at it like that." He smirked as his sister walked over and stood near the fire.

"I like your cousin," Bella said to Sarah.

"Thank you. You're all welcome to stay." She moved the blankets aside. "I guess I'd better go over and make sure none of my mother's yoga friends take your rooms tonight."

"I'll go with you." Ben stood.

"That'd be fine." She started towards the door. "Rowan," she called out, "we'll be right back."

"Take your time." He walked in from the back of the kitchen. "Dinner's almost ready. There's enough for everyone. Then you can head over after the classes are done."

Sarah stopped just inside the door and then walked over and wrapped her arms around her cousin. "Thank you."

Ben watched the man kiss the top of her head, much like he'd always done to Bella's.

"Anytime," he answered.

When they stepped outside in the cold, he glanced down. "You forgot your jacket." He frowned as he removed his coat and placed it on her shoulders.

"It shouldn't be cold, but it is." She frowned as she glanced up at the sky. "Normally now it's warmer.

"It's supposed to warm up later this week."

"It's the last chill." She sighed, her breath puffing out.

He took her hand as they started walking across the street. "I'm sorry I didn't tell you everything."

"No, it's okay. I understand. You can't go against your boss's wishes."

He stopped her just outside the gate. "Honestly, I didn't

know he was your grandfather or any of it until a few days ago."

"You came to Silver Cove to check up on me. Not to see if you wanted the job as manager?"

He dipped his head, keeping his eyes on hers.

"And?" she asked.

He held in a chuckle. "You're more than fit to take over the running of East Haven."

"But?" She tilted her head and looked at him.

"But, I put it in my report that I couldn't guarantee you'd be ready to run Elite International."

She was silent for a while. "I agree. I don't know the first thing about running a large business like that."

"What will you do?" he asked.

She wrapped her arms around him and pulled him close. "Looks like I'll have to hire someone to run the business for me. Someone I can keep my eye on."

"Oh yeah?" His arms went around her waist, holding her as tight as he could.

"Then we're in agreement." He waited as her smile grew. "Bella is going to run Elite International."

His bark of laughter echoed in the streets. Then he leaned down and kissed her lips, holding onto that moment for as long as he could.

After talking quickly with her mother and making sure the rooms would be free, they headed back over to Rowan's.

They enjoyed the dinner that Rowan made. Apparently, he had learned how to cook working in the kitchen at East Haven before leaving for college.

Before Ben followed Sarah up the stairs to her rooms, he'd made sure that his sister was settled on the second floor. They had called their parents together, telling them where they were and how long they were staying.

Bella begged them to allow her enough time to visit the school the next day. To the surprise of both them, they had agreed.

Sarah texted Lilith, asking her to cover for her over the next few days and promising to fill her friend in on everything once she returned back to work.

"What are you going to do?" he asked once they were alone in her room.

"What do you mean?" She turned to him, leaning against the back of the sofa.

"Well, after everything is settled, you won't have to work at the resort anymore." He fisted his hands and shoved them in his pockets, not trusting himself to stay away from her until they could finish the conversation that he knew had to happen.

She'd looked at him like he'd just kicked her. "Of course, I'll work there. It's what I love. It's my life."

He'd smiled at her. She was truly a remarkable woman. Her determination was one of the reasons he'd fallen so fast for her.

"What?" she asked.

"You're amazing," he added.

"Because I love my job?"

"No, because you love your job enough that you don't care how much money you have sitting in a bank. Nothing is going to keep you from doing what you love."

She frowned over at him. "Why would it?"

He moved closer to her, stopping short of touching her. "You've met my folks."

She nodded and he could tell she was holding her

breath.

"They aren't the kind of people that know what it means to work for something they love. Even though my father hounded it into me my entire life—honor, integrity, loyalty—the man wouldn't know the true meaning of those three words if they rose up out of the ground and slapped him in the face." He shook his head in disgust.

Her chuckled stopped him.

"Your father may not, but he raised two children that know exactly what those three words mean." She moved to him, wrapping her arms around his shoulders. "You showed me honor when you came to the resort and interviewed my employees, telling me you wouldn't get rid of Rodney even though he was older than most men doing his job. You showed me integrity when you kept your promise to keep my grandfather's secret from me, no matter what. And you have shown nothing but loyalty towards your sister. Even if it meant going against your parents' wishes." She leaned up and placed her lips on his.

"There's one more item I wish to discuss with you."

"What would that be?" she asked.

"Love." The word echoed in the silent room.

"Ben," she finally said, "I'm…"

"No, hear me out. We've come a long way and in such a short time. I've already turned in my resignation with Carl."

"You?" She stepped back again. "Why would you resign?"

"Because the job is in Boston and you are here." He moved to her, taking her into his arms. "And, since I want to be near the woman I love, it only makes sense."

"You…" He felt her arms start to shake. "I didn't

expect…"

"No, I can see you didn't," he broke in as he brushed a strand of her hair away from her face.

"Wait." She pulled back slightly. "Just wait. Let me finish. I didn't expect to feel this way about you either." His heart skipped. "I guess it was the way you fell at my feet the first time you saw me." She smiled as he chuckled. Her smile fell away. "But somewhere in between then and now, you've stolen my heart." Then she shook her head quickly. "No, not stolen, you won it. You have my heart."

"Sarah…" He pulled her closer and ran his lips over hers slowly. "What happens to us now?" he asked as he placed a kiss on the top of her head, silently wishing they weren't down the hallway from her mother.

"Now, I take over running East Haven, you take over Elite and learn how to work remotely, or we move the base of operations here." She pulled back. "Then we look for our own place to live in Silver Cove. That is…"—her smile grew— "after you buy me a ridiculously large wedding ring. And then…"—she leaned back further and smiled up at him— "we live happily ever after."

"I like your line of thinking." He frowned. "There's just one problem with it."

She frowned back at him. Then he took a step back, dipped down onto one knee, and took her hand in his. "This is how it's supposed to happen." He took her hand up to his lips. "Serenity Holley, would you marry me, so we can live happily ever after?"

Her smile grew as she nodded. "Of course, I will." Then she jumped into his arms as he spun her around and they both laughed loudly, not caring that there was a houseful of their family to hear them.

CHAPTER 23

There was little that Sarah dreaded in life, now. Dealing with her mother's ex-boyfriend, Joe was still top of her list.

But since she was packing up her stuff for the last time, she made an exception and tolerated him, especially since Ben was sitting across from her, smiling at her like he'd just won the best race in the world.

Even Lilith seemed to not mind that Joe was currently complaining about everything. For a yoga instructor, Joe was a downer. Even her mother had rolled her eyes several times while listening to him complain about working too much.

"Joe, why don't you run down to the kitchen and make us some green tea?" Crystal asked. When the man left the room, Sarah glanced over at her mother and shook her head.

"What?" Crystal said, shrugging her shoulders.

"How much longer are you going to keep him around?" Rowan asked, breaking the silence in the room.

Lilith giggled but turned quickly and disappeared into the bathroom. Sarah wanted to follow her friend, but her legs had fallen asleep and she didn't think she could move fast enough without the full blood flow.

"I don't see that that's any of your..." Crystal sighed when a loud curse traveled up the stairs as Joe banged into something on the way down. "Not long," she answered. "I don't know what has gotten into him lately. Ever since you took over running the resort and moved in with Ben," Crystal smiled happily as Ben reached over to take Sarah's hand.

"Don't forget we're engaged." Ben held up her hand, showing off the beautiful floral-motif ring on her finger.

"Yes, of course." Crystal's smile grew bigger. "I just can't believe you're leaving me." She heard her mother sniffle and scooted over until she could wrap her arms around her shoulders.

"We're just moving two blocks away." She felt her own eyes water.

"It might as well be two states." Crystal pulled back. "I guess I'm just emotional and in need of a cleansing." She took several deep breaths and Sarah knew she was releasing all the negative energy caused by Joe. "There, I feel better already." She smiled. "Now, how about we finish packing up, so you can get into your new place."

It took the rest of the afternoon and all five of them to finish packing up her room. Joe made a quick exit after getting everyone drinks.

Once all her boxes and larger items were dropped off at their new home, everyone disappeared, leaving her and Ben to sort through the mess.

"Can you believe it's ours?" She sighed as she leaned

back on their new sofa. They had gone shopping early last week for some of the odds and ends that were missing like the sofa and chairs, a dining room table and chairs, a king-size bed, and nightstands. The rest, they agreed, would have to come when they had more time.

"I knew you'd love it the moment I saw the place." He pulled her close and kissed the top of her head.

"Of course I love the place. I've been going by it all my life." She rested back against him, enjoying the feel of his chest rising and falling against hers. "It did help that the previous owners had just spent almost a year remodeling it." She glanced around the two-story Victorian home. The new hardwood floors shined in the dying sunlight. She could just imagine thick rugs placed in choice spots—one at the main entrance, another at the base of the staircase, and one in front of the massive fireplace. She couldn't keep from imagining the two of them making love for hours in front of a crackling fire on a cold night.

"Happy?" Ben asked, next to her ear.

"Very." She sighed, just as her stomach growled loudly. Ben chuckled.

"How about some pizza?" Ben started to get up.

"That sounds perfect, but you sit. I'll call in the order." She jumped up. Since the weather had taken a turn towards hot, she cracked a few windows as she made her way back to the newly remodeled kitchen.

She still got a rush when she walked into the large room. Soft colors, straight simple lines, and warmth. The room was perfect.

After ordering their favorite pizza, she leaned against the bar and let her mind wander over what the next few years would hold for them in this house. Would they have kids? When? How many?

"Lost in thought?" Ben's voice broke into her thoughts, almost causing her to jump.

Chuckling, she turned and wrapped her arms around him. "Yes." She leaned up on her toes and placed a soft kiss on his lips.

"About?" His arms around her felt wonderful.

"This place, us, the future."

"And?" He waited.

"Do you want kids?" she blurted out.

He leaned back until his eyes met hers. "You?"

She shook her head quickly. "Oh no, you don't. You don't get to avoid answering by turning it around on me. Do you want kids?" she asked again, biting her bottom lip as she waited for his answer.

Slowly, his smile returned. "I was thinking of having three. You?"

She smiled. "I was thinking of two. One of each."

He shook his head. "Take it from me, sometimes you need a third one in the mix to even things out." She giggled. "And they have to be close in age. No waiting too long in between."

She nodded. "Agreed."

His hands moved to her hips and pulled her up until she sat on the edge of the countertop. "So, when were you thinking of starting this family?" he asked as his lips trailed over her collarbone.

"Hmm." She moaned and tilted her chin, giving him better access. "Soon."

"How soon?" His mouth caused goose bumps to raise over her skin. "Like, how soon?" His hands dipped under her shirt. His fingers brushed against her sensitive skin as he started to unfasten her bra.

"I'll let you know…" She sighed. "After the pizza." She skirted aside and escaped his hold, laughing as he chased her into the living room.

They sat out on the front porch and enjoyed their pizza and a cold beer, then he carried her up the stairs and gently laid her on their new bed.

"I don't think I'll ever get used to seeing you like this," he moaned next to her skin once she was completely naked underneath him. "How beautiful you are." His fingers brushed over her skin softly. "How soft." He ran a finger up the side of her ribs. "How your eyes heat when I touch you and the sexy noises you make when I do this." His mouth covered her breast and she couldn't hold back the moan that escaped her lips.

"I know we talked about having a fall wedding, but I was thinking." She bit her bottom lip as he continued to excite her.

"Hmm?" he dipped lower. She shifted her hips and wrapped her legs around his waist, getting his full attention.

"Why don't we push up the wedding date to July?"

He stopped his movement and glanced up at her. "Can everything be ready in time?"

"I don't see why not. I mean, look at how fast we closed on this place."

"Sarah, that's less than a month away. Are you sure?"

She nodded, then tugged on him until he covered her again. "Besides, I happen to have some of the best wedding planning staff in the state working for me. I've already talked to—"

"Okay," he broke in, stopping her.

"Really?" She blinked and held still.

"Sure, I mean, the sooner the better." He smiled. "If it was up to me, I would marry you right this minute."

She laughed. "No, I still want a dress and flowers and—"

"I get it. So, pick a day. Let's do this." His hand moved down and covered her, sending all thoughts of their wedding out of her mind. "Now, if you're done talking…" He moved his fingers and she arched her back and gasped. "There's another business to tend to right this moment."

Lilith stood on the large boulder, occasionally glancing out at the vast open space behind her. She didn't think there was a more perfect day than today. Not when she glanced around and saw her best friend, Sarah, walking towards them in a white flowing dress. The off-the-shoulder vintage dress was perfect for Sarah's wedding. And the ring of flowers her mother had made for her hair really accented the natural feel of their wedding.

There were over three dozen guests standing on the large boulder face at the top of the hill. As Sarah walked towards them, soft music played from two speakers set up near the back.

Glancing over, she smiled at the way Ben watched his bride walk towards him. He looked so handsome in his tan cotton suit with his hiking boots. His best man, Rowan, stood off to the side, looking just as dashing.

Lilith, for her part, was dressed in a soft pink version of Sarah's dress, but a tad shorter. Underneath both of their dresses were matching hiking boots, so they could easily climb the hill to the wedding spot.

As the preacher started talking, Lilith's eyes roamed over the crowd. She didn't know Ben's family, but his parents didn't look too thrilled to be hosting the wedding in the wide open. Ben's sister, Bella, looked beyond thrilled. Actually, she looked the happiest out of all the guests. She too had flowers in her hair, which Lilith and Crystal had arranged.

Then her eyes landed on Adam Carriveau and her heart skipped a beat. Her eyes narrowed as she took in everything about him. The man had been put on earth just to torture her.

Quickly, before he could notice her looking at him, she turned her head away. The rest of the ceremony, she tried not to imagine his eyes on her, but she knew that he was watching her. She could feel her body heat under his gaze.

When Sarah and Ben finally kissed, the small crowd erupted into loud cheers. Lilith took Rowan's arm and walked back down the hillside with him, chatting with him about his latest job. The man was a doctor. And a damn sexy one at that.

Why did she feel so comfortable around him, but felt like her entire body was on fire around Adam? Both men were tall, blond, sexy, blue-eyed, and were in professional careers. Maybe it was because Adam did everything he could to just plain irritate her?

Since the first day working at East Haven Resorts, Adam had said and done things to get in her way.

If customers asked for substitutions on food items, he'd treat her like it was her idea. Every time he talked to her, he'd lay on the thick French accent, even though she'd overheard him talking to Sarah or one of the other staff members without it.

Once, she'd walked into the kitchen as he was talking with one of the waiters, and he'd been telling the guy that any woman he dated had better conform to his wishes and do everything in her power to please him. She'd gotten so pissed, she'd actually dropped a glass, causing the pair to realize that she'd been eavesdropping on them. Instead of getting embarrassed, he'd just smiled at her like he'd known she was there all along.

Then, there was the time he'd kissed her… She started to close her eyes, but then remembered they weren't all the way down the hill yet. She stumbled slightly, but Rowan's arm rushed around her and steadied her.

"Thanks," she mumbled.

"It's probably hard to hike in a long dress," he said, shifting her weight so that he took most of it.

"No, not really. I guess I was just lost in thought," she admitted.

"About?" His blue eyes bore into hers.

She was not going to open up to Rowan about Adam, so she lied. "I'm going to miss Sarah. I know they're only going to be gone on their honeymoon for a few weeks, but…" She let the rest drop.

"From what I hear, you're more than capable of handling things at the resort."

"Sure I am." She smiled, remembering how Sarah had given her a raise and the title of co-general manager. "I meant on a personal level." She sighed. "I feel like things are going to change now," she said, sidestepping a puddle of water.

"She's still going to be the same old Serenity, Rowan

added, causing Lilith to giggle. "What?" He helped her the rest of the way down the path.

"It's still so funny to hear her called that." She shook her head.

"The only family calls her that," Rowan said, stopping at the mouth of the trial as the other guests walked by them.

"Yes, I know, but..." She stopped when someone bumped into her from behind.

"Sorry." The French accent was thick this time. "I don't think we've met." Adam held out his hand to Rowan. "I'm Adam Carriveau."

"Rowan Holley, I'm Ser... Sarah's cousin," he corrected as he shook Adam's hand.

"Oh, oui. I've heard so much about you."

"As have I about you. I haven't made it out to the resort to enjoy one of your meals yet."

"No need to, I was put in charge of the dinner tonight." His eyes moved to Lilith's and she felt her spine straighten. "You are coming, oui?" His blue eyes bore into her own.

"Yes," Rowan answered, causing Adam to glance over at the forgotten man.

"Bien, I will see you there." Adam's eyes moved once more to Lilith's. "Lilly," he whispered, then turned and walked away.

"What was that all about?" Rowan leaned closer and whispered next to her ear.

She shivered slightly and knew it had nothing to do with Rowan's breath on her face. "He's conceited," she answered, a little too loudly. She heard Adam chuckle as he walked away and felt her face heat.

She was determined to have a good time for her friend but knew it was going to be next to impossible if Adam was going to constantly be underfoot for the rest of the night.

"Well, shall we?" Rowan held out his arm, waiting for her to take it.

Just then, Adam glanced back towards them as he stopped in front of his car. Pasting on a smile, she glanced over at Rowan and took his arm and followed him to his car. Since she'd ridden with Sarah and her mother, she figured riding with Rowan to the reception would be just the trick she needed to prove to Adam that the kiss between them had meant nothing.

FRENCH KISS

Lilith has one simple job for the next few weeks—to act as general manager for East Haven Resort, one of the most prestigious, high-dollar resorts along the Maine coast. Simple, right? Well, everything would have gone smoothly, if it weren't for the cocky, self-centered Frenchman who was in charge of the kitchen.

Adam has tried to deny his attraction for the sexy auburn-haired goddess long enough. Now that their boss is away on her honeymoon, it seems like the right time to stir things up. But when someone tries to snake in on his recent claim, he might just have to step up his game to win the prize he desires.

SILVER LINING

PRINT ISBN: 978-1-942896-65-4

DIGITAL ISBN: 978-1-942896-13-5

Copyeditor: Erica Ellis – inkdeepediting.com

The Pride Series

Finding Pride

Discovering Pride

Returning Pride

Lasting Pride

Serving Pride

Red Hot Christmas

My Sweet Valentine

Return To Me

Rescue Me

The Secret Series

Secret Seduction

Secret Pleasure

Secret Guardian

Secret Passions

Secret Identity

Secret Sauce

The West Series

Loving Lauren

Taming Alex

Holding Haley

Missy's Moment

Breaking Travis

Roping Ryan

Wild Bride

Corey's Catch

Tessa's Turn

The Grayton Series

Last Resort

Someday Beach

Rip Current

In Too Deep

Swept Away

High Tide

Lucky Series

Unlucky In Love

Sweet Resolve

Best of Luck

A Little Luck

Silver Cove Series

Silver Lining

French Kiss

Happy Accident

Hidden Charm

A Silver Cove Christmas

Entangled Series – Paranormal Romance

The Awakening

The Beckoning

The Ascension

Haven, Montana Series

Closer to You

Never Let Go

Holding On

Pride Oregon Series

A Dash of Love

My Kind of Love

Season of Love

Tis the Season

Dare to Love

Where I Belong

Wildflowers Series

Summer Nights

Summer Heat

Stand Alone Books

Twisted Rock

For a complete list of books:

http://JillSanders.com

Jill Sanders is a New York Times, USA Today, and international bestselling author of Sweet Contemporary Romance, Romantic Suspense, Western Romance, and Paranormal Romance novels. With over 55 books in eleven series, translations into several different languages, and audiobooks there's plenty to choose from. Look for Jill's bestselling stories wherever romance books are sold or visit her at jillsanders.com

Jill comes from a large family with six siblings, including an identical twin. She was raised in the Pacific Northwest and later relocated to Colorado for college and a successful IT career before discovering her talent for writing sweet and sexy page-turners. After Colorado, she decided to move south, living in Texas and now making her home along the Emerald Coast of Florida. You will find that the settings of several of her series are inspired by her time spent living in these areas. She has two sons and off-set the testosterone in her house by adopting three furry little ladies that provide her company while she's locked in her writing cave. She enjoys heading to the beach, hiking, swimming, wine-tasting, and pickleball with her husband, and of course writing. If you have read any of her books, you may also notice that there is a love of food, especially sweets! She has been blamed for a few added pounds by her assistant, editor, and fans… donuts or pie anyone?

facebook.com/JillSandersBooks

twitter.com/JillMSanders

bookbub.com/authors/jill-sanders

www.ingramcontent.com/pod-product-compliance
Lightning Source LLC
Chambersburg PA
CBHW060243210726